One of today's top contemporary romance writers, **Jayne Ann Krentz** has an astounding twelve million copies of her books in print. Her novels regularly appear on bestseller lists, including the *New York Times*. She is an innovative writer who has delved into psychic elements, intrigue, fantasy, historicals and even futuristic romances.

Jayne Ann Krentz lives in Seattle with her husband.

Also available from
Jayne Ann Krentz
in MIRA® Books

TEST OF TIME
THE TIES THAT BIND
CHANCE OF A LIFETIME
THE PRIVATE EYE
THE FAMILY WAY
LEGACY
FULL BLOOM

JAYNE ANN KRENTZ

Joy

MIRA® BOOKS

*First published in Great Britain 1989
This edition published 1997 by
MIRA Books, Eton House, 18-24 Paradise Road,
Richmond, Surrey, TW9 1SR*

© Jayne Ann Krentz 1988

ISBN 1 55166 062 8

58-9709

Printed and bound in Great Britain

Joy

ONE

Angus Cedric Ryerson, known as A. C. Ryerson to his business associates, Ryerson to his friends and as A.C. to no one who wished to remain on speaking terms with the man, studied the narrow, twisting road ahead. He swore softly and with great depth of feeling. What there was of the pavement was just barely visible through the pouring rain that was hitting the windshield with an unrelenting rhythm.

Ryerson decided that there was only one major drawback to being stood up by Deborah Middlebrook: he was not getting the chance to indulge the enormous sense of relief he was feeling.

At this moment he should have been sitting in front of a comforting fire, taking further comfort from a glass of good Scotch. He ought to have been allowed to listen to the storm while savoring Mozart and twelve-year-old liquor. It seemed only fair that he be free to wallow happily in his abject misery. Given the circumstances, it was a reasonable expectation. A man who got stood up on the eve of a weekend with a desirable woman deserved a little consideration while he mourned his loss.

Ryerson slowed the silver Mercedes for another hairpin turn and then swore again as he had to decrease his speed even more to negotiate a deep puddle in a dip in the road. Instead of enjoying a fire, a glass of Scotch and Mozart he was driving through one of the worst storms that had struck the Pacific Northwest all year. It was early May. Spring was supposed to be bursting into bloom.

As if the lousy weather weren't sufficient punishment, he was laboring to find a vague address in a rural location on an island where no one spent much money on street signs. At the rate he was going, he would be lucky to find his way back to the ferry terminal before the last boat left for Seattle.

He had only himself to blame for his present situation. Discovery of Debby's note had left him awash in relief. He should have quit while he was ahead and retired at once to his Scotch and Mozart.

Unfortunately Debby's parents had learned that their daughter had fled. They had panicked, afraid their youngest might do something reckless while in the throes of despair from a disintegrating love affair.

Ryerson had made one or two attempts to assure the Middlebrooks that Debby was in full command of herself, but they had not been convinced. He had then attempted to explain as delicately as possible that the love affair they thought was going up in flames had in reality never generated more than a little mild smoke. The Middlebrooks had ignored that bit of reassurance, too.

He'd definitely been a bit too delicate in his explanations. But it was difficult to tell a pleasant, rather old-fashioned couple such as the Middlebrooks that you weren't sleeping with their youngest daughter. To bring the subject up at all suggested one had seriously considered sleeping with their dear darling and that led to additional difficult explanations.

In the end Ryerson had taken pity on John and Leona Middlebrook. He had been feeling so relieved to be free of Debby that he had rashly volunteered to find her and make certain she was safe.

It had been a mistake. John and Leona had immediately taken him up on his offer, gratitude reflected on their worried faces. Too late, Ryerson had realized there had been something besides parental gratitude in their eyes. He was sure he'd also seen a heavy dose of hopeful expectation. He wished now that he'd kept his mouth shut. It was no secret the Middlebrooks had been hoping that the romance between Debby and Ryerson would evolve into something more substantial.

Something as substantial as marriage, to be exact.

Ryerson couldn't blame them. He'd had a few fleeting thoughts in that direction himself in the beginning. Marriage to Debby had seemed eminently logical at one point. Luckily he had come to his senses.

As he fought the storm, Ryerson reminded himself that sooner or later a man paid for his good luck. He was paying the price tonight.

The consensus, after the obvious places had been checked, was that Debby had probably gone to stay at her sister's island home. A phone call had produced no answer, and the Middlebrookses' assumption was that, owing to her emotional distress, Debby wasn't answering the phone. The sister, Ryerson was told, was out of town.

The only solution that would reassure everyone was for Ryerson to take the ferry from downtown Seattle to the island, locate Debby and demonstrate to all concerned that she was in good condition and not indulging in a fit of hysterics or crying inconsolably.

For their sakes Ryerson hoped the Middlebrooks were not harboring too many false expectations about a grand reconciliation. Having escaped Debby once by the skin of his teeth, Ryerson had no intention of getting tangled up again with her. She was a very charming, very attractive young woman, but another week or two of her company would have driven him over the edge.

The road curved again and a small, slanted signpost flashed briefly in the glare of the headlights. Ryerson remembered the directions John Middlebrook had written down for him and turned the wheel of the Mercedes to the right. The road narrowed again, a mere path between towering pines.

Ryerson wondered once more about the mysterious sister whose cottage he was trying to find tonight. Whoever she was, she had the same taste in real estate that he had. His own weekend retreat was farther north but the surroundings were similar. His place was con-

siderably more remote, however. It was on a tiny dot
of an island in the San Juans and could only be reached
by boat. At least Virginia Elizabeth Middlebrook had
ferry service to her island.

Virginia Elizabeth. The name made him think of
royalty. There was an old-fashioned dignity about it
that appealed to him. Other than the fact that she was
a few years older than Debby, which made her about
thirty-three, Ryerson knew almost nothing about this
sister. Somehow they had always managed to miss
meeting. Lately he knew Virginia Elizabeth had been
out of town a lot. Something to do with her job as an
information retrieval manager.

Ryerson was reminding himself that he wasn't going
to meet her tonight, either, because she was still out of
town, when the cottage came into view. He could see
little of it in the headlights, but from what he could tell,
it was a comfortable-looking older home nestled in the
trees near the water's edge. Lights glowed warmly in the
windows.

Ryerson would have been happier to see the cheerfully lit windows if he hadn't known it meant he'd finally tracked Debby to her lair. He parked the Mercedes
in the drive and switched off the ignition. Then he sat
for a moment, measuring the distance he would have
to cross in the rain before he reached the shelter of the
porch.

There was no help for it. He was going to get wet no
matter how fast he sprinted to the steps. The umbrella
was in the trunk, naturally. By the time he got it out,

he would be soaked. Might as well head straight for the cottage.

Ryerson was the kind of man who did not put off the inevitable. Thinking wistfully of Scotch, a warm fire, Mozart and the esoteric joys of celibacy, he opened the car door and loped toward the porch.

He didn't stand a chance against the driving rain. His expensive tweed jacket was soaked by the time he reached shelter and his heavy wing-tip shoes were water stained.

Irritated and resigned to his fate, Ryerson leaned heavily on the doorbell. The sooner this little confrontation was over, the better. All he wanted to do was go home. Alone.

VIRGINIA ELIZABETH MIDDLEBROOK had just stepped out of the shower when the doorbell rang. She paused in the act of wrapping her wet hair in a towel and listened intently. The bell rang again. She frowned. She was certainly not expecting anyone tonight. No one knew she had returned a day early.

It might be a neighbor who needed something and had seen that the lights were on in her cottage, she told herself. Perhaps the Burtons down the road had lost their power because of the storm and needed candles.

Still, a woman living alone could not be too careful. Virginia tightened the sash of her comfortable old terry-cloth robe, tucked in the towel to form a turban for her damp hair and went down the hall to the living room. Her fluffy pink mules flopped comfortably against the aging hardwood floor.

The doorbell chimed once more. There was a distinctly impatient sound to it this time, she decided.

"Who is it?" she asked firmly, and simultaneously put her eye to the tiny glass peephole set in the door. She could see nothing except a broad male shoulder. The shoulder appeared to be covered in wet tweed.

"It's Ryerson. Who the hell do you think it is?" a man's voice growled back from the other side of the door. "Open up, Debby. Your parents are worried sick, and I'm cold and wet. Let's get this scene over so I can go home and languish in peace."

Virginia blinked and stepped back from the door. Ryerson. The name was very familiar because a man named Ryerson had recently bought her father's business. She thought there were initials connected to the name, although she couldn't recall them.

This must be the same Ryerson her sister had mentioned once or twice on the phone, the man Debby had been dating recently. He did not sound happy. Nor did he sound like a doting lover. What in the world had Debby done this time, Virginia wondered.

Tentatively she unlocked the door and opened it. She eyed the large, damp male on her doorstep with considerable misgiving. She had to look up some distance to meet his eyes, an unusual experience for her. Virginia Elizabeth was five feet nine inches in her stocking feet. A quick first estimate put her sister's current boyfriend somewhere in the vicinity of six two—a very solid six two. That same assessing glance told her that *boyfriend* was definitely a misnomer. This man was pushing forty if he was a day, and he looked as if he'd gotten there the hard way.

The missing initials popped into her head. A.C.

It was obvious that A. C. Ryerson was not thrilled to find himself standing where he was at that hour of the night. The harsh glow of the yellow porch light revealed an aggressive, severe jawline and high cheekbones. His eyes glinted at her as they swept her from the top of her toweled head to the toes of her worn, fluffy slippers.

"You're not Debby."

"No, I'm not," she retorted, uncomfortably aware of her freshly scrubbed condition. Freshly scrubbed looked great at eighteen, but at thirty-three it wasn't quite so cute. "I'm Virginia Elizabeth. You're A. C. Ryerson?"

"The last time I checked my driver's license. Is Debby here?"

"No."

"Good." He appeared unduly pleased by the information.

Virginia was taken aback. "I just got home a couple of hours ago. She's definitely not here, and there's no sign that she has been. Why? What's wrong?"

"Nothing as far as I'm concerned, but your folks are frantic. Mind if I come in, or shall I explain everything while I get shrink-wrapped by my jacket?"

Virginia smiled ruefully. "Sorry. Come on in. As you can see, I just got out of the shower. I was about to have a nightcap and go to bed. I've been stuck in airplanes and airports since six o'clock this morning."

"I know the feeling," Ryerson said as he came through the door. "It takes a while to unwind. I would be forever grateful if you would allow me to join you. I've got some unwinding of my own to do."

Virginia's eyes widened in genuine shock. "Join me?"

"In the nightcap. Not bed," he said gently.

Heat rushed into her cheeks. It was an odd sensation. She hadn't blushed in ages. "Oh, yes, of course. Sorry about that. I'm a little groggy. Please sit down," she waved him hastily toward the sofa. "I'll get you something. What do you drink?"

"I've been fantasizing about a glass of Scotch for the past two hours." Ryerson wandered toward the fireplace and examined the supply of kindling. "There was a fire in my fantasy, too. Any objections if I build one? I'm soaked."

Virginia stared at him in astonishment. "Go ahead. Your fantasy life sounds quite tame."

"I assure you it is. I'm a simple man with simple fantasies."

Virginia blushed again under the speculative expression in his silver-gray eyes. "Here, I'll take your jacket."

He shrugged out of it willingly enough, revealing a conservative white shirt and a sedately striped tie. Not at all the sort of clothes she would have expected one of Debby's dates to wear. Virginia put the equally conservative-looking jacket over the back of a chair. "I'll, uh, see if I have any Scotch." She retreated to the kitchen.

Something very strange was going on here, Virginia decided as she located an old, dusty bottle of Scotch and poured a hefty shot into a large glass. She eyed the level of liquid in the glass and added another splash. A. C. Ryerson was a large man.

She was surprised by his massiveness. It gave him an air of granite-hard solidity that was unusual in Debby's male acquaintances who generally tended toward the slender, more devil-may-care sorts. Ryerson was also older than most of Debby's boyfriends. Debby, a vivacious twenty-four, tended to stick to men who were closer to her own age. They were easier to manage, Debby had once explained.

There were a few other things that surprised Virginia about A. C. Ryerson. He appeared to be a good deal more grim and hard than Virginia would have guessed. Definitely not Debby's typical yuppie type. Debby liked her men trendy and adventurous. She preferred the kind of man who liked to dance to hard rock until two in the morning and spend the next day partying on a boat in the middle of Lake Washington.

Virginia had a strong hunch A. C. Ryerson was not the type to routinely rock around the clock.

She poured herself a glass of wine and went back into the living room with both drinks. It was time for a few explanations.

Ryerson was on one knee in front of the fireplace. He had a small blaze going and was feeding it carefully. She saw that he had loosened his tie. He glanced up as Virginia came forward with the Scotch. Reaching for it with obvious gratitude he took one long swallow.

"Thank you," he said heavily. "I needed that."

"You're welcome."

Virginia sat down on the couch and put her wine on the table in front of her. She watched Ryerson as he carefully placed one more log on the fire and then got to his feet. *A very big man*, she thought again. But it was all lean, muscled strength. There was no softness about his hard frame. *Comfortably, reassuringly large.* Immediately she wondered what had put the words into her brain. Other than her father, she seldom thought of men as being either comfortable or reassuring.

Ryerson started toward the couch and then halted as he caught sight of the compact-disc player on a table. He paused beside the collection of discs long enough to select some Mozart and drop it into the player. When the crystal strains of a piano concerto floated liltingly into the room, Ryerson nodded in satisfaction and sat down at the opposite end of the sofa. His weight put a considerable dent in the cushions.

"To narrow escapes," he said, stretching his legs out in front of him. He toasted the fire with his Scotch.

"Who or what, precisely, have you just escaped from, Mr. Ryerson?" Virginia asked a little tartly.

"A weekend of unmitigated debauchery." He looked at her through lazily narrowed eyes. "Call me Ryerson, by the way. All my friends do. Nobody except my mother calls me by my first or second names."

"Which are?"

"Angus Cedric."

"Hmm. I can see why you don't use them much. They're nice names, though. A little old-fashioned but solid and substantial."

"And dull?" he suggested helpfully.

"No, not at all," she said quickly, startled at the thought. *Dull* was the last word that came to mind when she looked at Ryerson, she realized in mild surprise.

"Thanks," he said dryly. "I'll stick with Ryerson. So you're Virginia Elizabeth?"

"That's right."

"You're not at all like your sister."

"So I've been told since she was in her cradle." Virginia sipped her wine and wondered where all this was leading. "Can I assume that you and my sister have had some sort of lovers' spat?"

"Spat?" Ryerson considered the word for a moment. "No, I wouldn't say that. More like a permanent parting of the ways. Your sister and I had planned to go away together this weekend. We both came to our senses and changed our minds at the last minute. Rest assured, it's a great relief to both of us."

Virginia groaned. "The big romance is over?"

"I'm afraid so."

"Mom and Dad are not going to be pleased."

"They aren't, but I am."

"Yes, I'm getting that feeling." Not at all the stricken, desperate, cast-off lover, she thought. But then, she doubted if this man would play that role for any woman.

"I don't mind telling you, it was a close call, Virginia Elizabeth." Ryerson took another swallow of Scotch and leaned his head back against the sofa. "A very close call. I'm still not quite sure how I let myself get this near to total disaster. Do you know I was even thinking about marriage in the beginning? I've been wondering for weeks how to get out of the mess, but your sister has kindly taken care of the situation herself. Apparently she had the good sense to panic, too. Unfortunately she made a scene out of what should have been a simple matter of saying no, thank you."

"My sister usually does things with a flourish."

"So I've learned. This time she left a note. I think I've got it here somewhere." Ryerson leaned over to pluck a damp piece of paper from his jacket pocket. "Here, read it for yourself."

Virginia quickly scanned the short note.

Ryerson, please forgive me, but I can't go through with it. It's all been a terrible mistake. I must have some time alone to think. I have come to the conclusion that it's all over between us. I'm sorry.

It was signed, "Debby."

"I fail to see the problem here," Virginia remarked. "Debby apparently declined your invitation to spend the weekend with her and you're happy she did. What's the difficulty?"

"Your parents are worried about her whereabouts and her state of mind." Ryerson spoke with acute disgust. "They seem to think she might be sinking into depression and despair."

"Debby? Not likely."

"I agree." Ryerson's dark brows rose slightly. "I think there's a bit more to it than that. Your parents were very happy when she started dating me. They are not at all pleased that the ship of love has foundered."

"Ah. Now that makes more sense. They encouraged you to go after her in the hopes that there might be a grand reconciliation, I'll bet."

"I think so."

"And is there a chance of that happening?" Virginia asked calmly.

"Not a chance in hell. The whole thing was a big mistake. She was right about that."

"I see. I'll bet you don't make many, do you?"

"Mistakes? No," he said blandly, "I don't."

She believed him. Virginia looked at the lean, solid length of him and then her eyes moved to his face. It was an interesting face, she decided. Not particularly good-looking, but definitely interesting. It was an over-whelmingly masculine face—all blunt, roughly carved planes and angles.

Ryerson's hair was still gleaming from the rain. The firelight revealed a hint of red in the thick brown depths. He caught her examining him and smiled faintly. His lazy, hooded gaze revealed a cool, faintly predatory intelligence.

Virginia could see curls of crisp hair where Ryerson's expensive white shirt was open at the collar. She stirred slightly, tucking her slippered feet under her old robe. She was aware of a faint restlessness in herself that was distinctly unusual. She knew the feeling was generated by Ryerson's presence, but she did not understand it. Once more her gaze slipped to the opening of his shirt.

"Wondering what your sister saw in me?" Ryerson asked mildly.

Virginia felt herself flushing again and wished she could have disguised her reaction. "Of course not."

He shrugged comfortably. "I do."

"I'll admit you're not quite her usual type," Virginia allowed cautiously.

"Thank God. Too bad it took us both so long to figure it out. All I can say in my own defense is that it seemed like a good idea at the time."

"I know my parents probably encouraged both of you to think it was a good idea," Virginia said with a smile. "Dad had visions of keeping the business in the family after he sold it. He and Mom thought it would be just ducky if you married Debby."

"Uh-huh."

"Mom and Dad sent you here looking for Debby?"

"When they couldn't locate her at her own apartment they assumed she must have come here. I, being innately gallant and noble, not to mention euphoric over my narrow escape, agreed to make certain she was okay. However, having come this far, I feel I've discharged my duty in the matter. I refuse to feel any further obligation."

"What about your male ego?" Virginia asked before stopping to think. "Isn't that involved?"

His mouth twisted derisively. "My ego will survive just fine, thank you. It's been through worse."

Virginia believed him when he said his ego would survive. There was something about this man that made her think his self-confidence ran deep and was

grounded in bedrock. It would take more than a flee-
ing girlfriend to shake it.

"So now that you've fulfilled your obligation, you're
going to turn around and drive back to Seattle?" Virginia asked curiously.

Ryerson cradled his glass in his big hands and stared
into the fire. "Right. Just as soon as I've dried out. I appreciate your hospitality, Virginia Elizabeth. I also appreciate the fact that you're not having hysterics or
screaming at me for what I've done to your sister."

"Have you done anything to my sister?"

Ryerson caught the underlying question in the words
and gave his hostess an assessing sidelong glance. "No,"
he said bluntly. "This was supposed to be the big weekend. The fact that we hadn't made it into bed before this
should have been an early tip-off, I suppose."

She looked at him in confusion. "I don't understand."

He grimaced. "Let's just say that after a month of
nothing more than a few uninteresting good-night
kisses, one has to assume there was little chance of a
grand passion developing at any time in the near future."

"Oh. I didn't mean that. It's certainly none of my
business!"

"Forget it." Ryerson grinned briefly at her obvious
embarrassment. "I only mention the subject because I
want to assure you that your sister and I are not all that
involved, in spite of the big plans for this weekend. My
fault, I admit."

"Your fault?" she echoed weakly. She stared at him in startled amazement.

Ryerson's grin came and went again. Virginia Elizabeth was good for his ego, he decided. The way she was looking at him implied she could not imagine him having any problems in the bedroom. His ego might not need continuous stroking to survive, but it was fully capable of luxuriating in this kind of attention when it got it.

"I never got up the energy to take her to bed," he said frankly. "Every time we got home from a date, either my ears were still ringing from an excess of loud rock music or I was exhausted from trying to keep up with her on the dance floor. I'm nearly forty years old, not twenty-five. I no longer attempt to party until two in the morning and then try to impress a woman in bed."

"But you were going away together this weekend?"

"I think the idea was a last-ditch effort on both our parts to inject a little vitality into a less-than-immortal love affair. I realized it wasn't worth the effort and was getting ready to tell her so when her famous note arrived."

"Not exactly a thrilling romance."

Ryerson looked at her. "A mistake all the way around. But it's over now. I can relax." He took another swallow of the good Scotch and let the soothing music sink into his bones as the warmth from the fire enveloped him. This was exactly what he needed, what he had been wanting all evening.

Virginia Elizabeth fitted her name, Ryerson decided as he savored the smoky Scotch. Tall, dignified, and wonderfully mature. She was taking his unexpected arrival and the news of her sister's disappearance with great calm. A woman of good sense and intelligence, he thought. Not at all like that flighty, scatterbrained sister of hers. A man could talk to Virginia Elizabeth, really talk to her.

She looked very cozy and comfortable sitting there at the other end of the sofa. Virginia Elizabeth was a fine-looking woman in many respects, he decided.

Ryerson found himself cataloging her assets. Good eyes, for a start. Beautiful eyes, in fact. They were hazel and at first glance seemed to suggest a quiet, womanly confidence. But there was a disturbing wariness, too, he noted.

The lines of her feminine jaw and straight, assertive nose were well defined. Her skin was pleasantly flushed from the fire.

He couldn't tell for certain what lay beneath the ancient terry-cloth robe, but he had an impression of full breasts and well-rounded hips. The woman had some shape to her, Ryerson thought with satisfaction. Not at all like her fashionably skinny sister. Virginia Elizabeth was built to keep a man warm in bed.

The stray sensual thought triggered a dull ache in his lower body that took Ryerson by surprise. He shifted slightly on the sofa, thinking it had been a very long time since he'd had to worry about spontaneous combustion.

"Well, I'm glad we're not going to be dealing with heartbreak and shattering disillusionment here," Virginia was saying briskly. "Could be a bit awkward, what with you just having bought out Dad's business and all."

"I think that might have been part of the problem as far as your sister was concerned," Ryerson said thoughtfully. "She seemed to like the idea of continuing financial security, but she did not care for the notion of being married to a man who was heavily into diesel generators and power systems."

Virginia laughed. "You've got to admit that a career in diesel generators and power systems lacks a certain sophisticated cachet. What made you decide to buy my father's business, anyway?"

"Middlebrook Power Systems is a solid, old-line firm that can be turned into a real money cow with the right management."

"And you're going to milk it?"

"All it needs is some capital poured into it for retooling and modernizing, and the sky's the limit. I've been involved with motors and power systems of one kind or another most of my life. I was the kind of kid who made a career out of shop classes in high school. Always had an after-school job at the local gas station. Then I spent a couple of years in the army, working on tanks and trucks until I finally wised up and went to college. There's more money in managing and consulting on power systems than there is in fixing them. As it happens, I found out I enjoyed the business end of things almost as much as the tinkering end. I know a good investment when I see it. When John Middlebrook put his firm on the block, I grabbed it."

"And my sister grabbed you," Virginia finished shrewdly.

Ryerson groaned. "You could put it that way. But I'm not sure how much of it was Debby's idea. Your parents were pushing her hard."

"I know. I can understand their motivations, but what about yours?"

Ryerson gazed into the fire. "I discovered I wasn't opposed to the idea. The fact is I wouldn't mind getting married again. Under the right circumstances marriage is a pleasant, comfortable institution."

"But, as someone once said, who wants to live in an institution?" Virginia remarked dryly. "To be fair, you may be right. From a man's point of view marriage probably does look pleasant and comfortable. But it looks different to a woman."

Ryerson glanced at her narrowly. "You surprise me. I thought most women wanted to get married, especially women over a, uh, certain age—" He broke off abruptly and grimaced.

"Especially women over thirty?" Virginia finished for him. "I'll let you in on a little secret. We're not all desperate." She shivered unconsciously. "I tried marriage once, and it was a disaster. I learn from my mistakes."

The depth of emotion in her voice caught Ryerson's full attention. "I was married once myself, and it didn't work out, but I'm willing to give it another try. I think marriage has definite possibilities if two people go into it with their eyes open, a set of reasonable expectations and a willingness to make a commitment."

"You believe that strongly in the power of love?" she asked in a soft voice.

"No," he said flatly. "I don't believe in love at all. Love is an artificial emotion. It's a twentieth-century fiction created for the fuzzy-brained romantics of this world, and I'm definitely not one of them. I do believe in marriage, however."

"Why?"

It struck Ryerson that this was a rather unusual conversation to be having with Debby's sister. But he found himself intrigued by it. "As I said, I think marriage has a lot to offer. The first time around for me I'll admit was a matter of raging hormones and youthful optimism. We were both too young, and neither of us had any reasonable expectations about marriage. She got restless and started wondering what she'd missed by marrying so young. I couldn't blame her. Things just fell apart. But next time for me will be different."

"Different?"

He nodded. "The next time around, I'll see to it that things are based on more solid, realistic foundations. I know what I want. I've reached the age when I value a comfortable, dependable home life. I guess I'm basically a home-and-hearth type. When I bought your dad's company and moved to Seattle from Portland, I felt as if I'd finally found what I wanted to do with the rest of my life. I felt as if I'd found the place where I wanted to live. I would like a nice, quiet, reliable, monogamous relationship to go along with all that. I'd like to marry someone I could count on. Someone to act as hostess when I entertain business associates. Someone who would share a drink with me in the evening while we talked about our day. I don't know what made me think even for a moment that it would be like that with Debby. I must have gone crazy."

"Either that or your hormones decided to get involved in the decision again," Virginia said with a smile.

"My hormones do nothing these days without my permission." Ryerson took another swallow of his Scotch and wondered about the truth of that statement. He could still feel the tautness in his groin. He wondered if she realized that the top of the terry-cloth robe was gaping slightly, just enough to give him a tantalizing glimpse of soft, rounded flesh.

"So you're willing to marry for comfort and convenience?"

"You sound disapproving."

She appeared to give that some thought. "Well, at least you're honest about it. In some ways I understand and agree with what you're saying. I wouldn't mind having a nice, reliable, stable friendship with a man. I get along very well by myself, but there are times when it would be fun to share things with someone. But I would never marry to get those things."

"You'd rather have an affair?" he asked with grave interest.

"I said it would be nice to have a comfortable friendship with a man. I don't know about an affair. I've never had one," she explained calmly. "I'm not sure I want one. But if I did have one, I would want it to be based on friendship, not hormones."

Ryerson was startled. He tried not to betray the reaction. "When were you divorced?" he asked.

"I wasn't. My husband died a few years ago."

Ryerson cleared his throat. "A few years ago?"

"I was married at twenty-five, and he died when I was twenty-seven. A car accident."

"And you've never... I mean in all this time you haven't gotten involved with, uh..." He let the sentence trail off, aware he was embarrassing her. But the truth was, it was difficult to imagine this woman having lived alone for so long.

"I've never found the kind of friendship that could be turned into a steady, dependable relationship," she answered quietly, "let alone someone I could fall in love with."

"You do believe in love, then?" he asked a little more sharply than he'd intended.

"Oh, yes. I believe in love, although I don't expect to ever find myself involved in a grand passion. I'm not the type. That's for people like my sister." Her mouth curved wryly. "I don't expect to fall in love. I much prefer the idea of a close friendship."

"And you would not want to marry this hypothetical friend?"

"Never in a million years."

Ryerson felt an irrational urge to argue the point. Then he relaxed and chuckled. "I believe in marriage but not love, and you believe in love but not marriage. Both of us agree about the importance of friendship, however. That's reassuring. It's also amusing when you think about it." His humor faded. "Your sister is still at the age when she expects fireworks and drama and a continuous good time."

"True."

"The fact is," Ryerson said as he sipped his drink, "I wasn't the kind of man who could have provided her with those things even when I was twenty-five. Maybe it has something to do with having made a career out of diesel motors and power systems. The field lacks a certain flashiness, and so do I. Do you realize there has been little change in the basic diesel power system in the past fifty years? The fundamental concept is steady, dependable and enduring."

Virginia grinned. "A tried-and-true product."

"Rather like marriage. It works beautifully as long as no one indulges in unrealistic expectations or makes too many demands. Was that your problem the first time around, Virginia Elizabeth? Did you go into marriage blinded by rose-colored glasses? Lord knows I did."

She stiffened, and anger flashed briefly in her hazel eyes. "I do not discuss my marriage with anyone outside my family."

Ryerson backed off immediately. He knew when he'd hit a brick wall. The easiest way to deal with brick walls was to go around them. He let the conversation lapse into silence.

"Now what?" Virginia asked after a few minutes of uneasy quiet. She was obviously anxious to change the subject.

Ryerson leaned back in his corner of the sofa and loosened another button on his shirt. He probably should be leaving, but somehow he didn't feel like making the effort. The Scotch was soothing, the music was delightful and the fire was comfortable. And if his hostess shifted her position just slightly, the gap in the front of her robe would widen another couple of inches. A man could not reasonably ask for much more out of an evening.

"I ought to be thanking you for your hospitality and seeing myself out the door," Ryerson observed aloud. But he didn't move.

Virginia glanced at the mantel clock. She hesitated for a few seconds and then said, "You've got an hour and a half until the last ferry sails."

"Plenty of time," he mused. "Now that I know my way it will only take fifteen minutes to get to the dock."

"Perhaps if you wait another forty-five minutes or so, the worst of this storm will pass. It's a nasty night for driving."

"Yes," Ryerson said. "It is. There was a regular lake forming across the road a mile or so from your turn-off."

"I know that section. It floods regularly. It can take hours to drain."

They both looked at the clock and another few moments of quiet, thoughtful silence prevailed.

"Why haven't I met you before, Virginia Elizabeth?" Ryerson eventually asked. "Your family mentioned you but said you were out of town a lot lately. I think they planned to introduce us at a dinner party next week. Do you do a lot of traveling?"

Virginia smiled and shook her head. "No, not under normal circumstances. I manage the computerized information-retrieval system for Carrington Miles and Associates. Do you know the company?"

He nodded. "Big conglomerate headquartered in Seattle. They've got business operations all over the Northwest."

"That's right. They're trying to standardize the information-retrieval systems at all their branches, and I've been assigned to oversee the standardization process. Hence the traveling. The job I just finished should be the last for quite a while, though. I think everything's under control."

Ryerson thought about that. "One of the things I want to modernize at Middlebrook Power Systems is the documentation control process. Maybe I should hire you as a consultant."

Virginia shook her head and chuckled. "The firm is hopelessly out of date in that area. Dad never saw the need to update his retrieval system."

She then surprised Ryerson by launching into an intelligent monologue on the wonders of modern computer-aided information systems. He found himself learning more than he really wanted to know on the subject, but somehow it was very easy to listen.

He interrupted finally to get himself some more Scotch. When he returned to the sofa he started talking about the plans he had for the future of Middlebrook Power Systems. Virginia was gratifyingly interested. Unfortunately she had adjusted the front of her robe while he was pouring his drink.

The fire blazed cheerfully, and the storm continued unabated. It wasn't until Ryerson had finished a lengthy, detailed description of his plans to open overseas markets for Middlebrook that Virginia again glanced at the mantel clock. Her eyes widened.

"You'll never make the last ferry," she said anxiously.

Ryerson followed her gaze. "Damn." But he made no move to grab his jacket and rush toward the door. "Maybe it's just as well, considering how much of your Scotch I've gone through."

Virginia frowned slightly. "There are a couple of bed-and-breakfast places on the island. You might try one."

"Good idea."

They both continued to sit and gaze into the fire as if seeking answers there. Virginia finally spoke up cautiously.

"There's no reason you can't stay here, as long as you don't mind spending the rest of the night on my sofa," she said. "It's a little small for you, but . . ."

"That's very kind of you, Virginia Elizabeth."

"Nonsense. After all, you're a good friend of the family, even if you and Debby have recently broken off the romance of the year."

He returned her smile. "I like to think so."

Forty minutes later, Ryerson found himself stretched out on the sofa with a fresh-smelling sheet, a wool blanket and a fluffy pillow. It was a tight fit, but he felt remarkably comfortable. The remains of the fire glowed on the hearth.

He listened to Virginia Elizabeth puttering around in the bedroom and then heard her turn out the light and climb into bed. He indulged himself in some pleasant fantasizing, picturing her in prim white underwear. She was the type to wear prim white underwear. Then he imagined her removing the underwear. When the mental pictures got too intense and the heavy, tight feeling in his lower body grew too uncomfortable, he told himself to go to sleep.

But the images didn't disappear completely, and Ryerson still had one in his head when he finally drifted into a deep slumber. It was the picture of a regally tall woman with full, ripe breasts and nicely rounded thighs reaching up to welcome him into her arms.

Ryerson's last conscious thought was that he had been dating the wrong sister for the past month.

TWO

Virginia awoke the next morning with the feeling that something rigid and unyielding in her life had been pushed permanently askew. It was a disconcerting sensation. She opened her eyes, gazed at the ceiling and wondered how having one very large male spend the night on her sofa could have any long-term effect on her quiet, well-ordered existence.

The answer was that she was imagining things. The event could not have any such effect. She had simply provided a bed to a business associate of her father's who also happened to be a friend of the family. End of adventure.

Irritated with herself, she threw back the covers, tugged on her robe and padded out of the bedroom and down the hall to the bathroom. It wasn't until she reached it that she realized it was already occupied. The shower was running full force. The experience of having to share her bathroom with a man was a novel one, to say the least. She went on toward the living room.

The pillow, blanket and sheet she had given Ryerson the previous evening had already been neatly folded and stored in the hall cupboard. Only a pair of very large wingtips neatly aligned on the floor and a white shirt hanging over the back of a chair gave evidence of a man's presence.

The shower went off and Virginia stilled, listening intently. She pictured Ryerson drying himself with one of her oversize white bath towels. When she found herself trying to decide if the pattern of his chest hair formed an arrow below his waist, she knew it was time to go start the coffee. Her imagination was definitely in high gear this morning. Very unusual for her.

A few minutes later, the bathroom door opened. Virginia concentrated on taking two cups out of the cupboard. She didn't hear Ryerson coming down the hall, which surprised her, given his size. But she sensed his presence in the doorway behind her.

"Good morning," he said quietly. His voice was deep and dark with a faint trace of morning huskiness that struck her as remarkably sexy.

Clutching the cups, Virginia turned around. "Good morning."

She hadn't been quite certain how he would appear to her this morning. But he turned out to be just as interesting in the early light as he had been last night in front of a fire. The fact that he was half-nude undoubtedly contributed to the overall fascination she acknowledged privately. It had been years since she'd had a half-nude man in her kitchen. The last one had been her husband, and she had no warm memories of either him or his nudity.

But Ryerson was something else again. His red-brown hair was gleaming from the shower, and his eyes appeared very silvery in the sunlight. He was wearing only his slacks, and Virginia realized that the hair on his chest followed exactly the pattern she had envisaged. It formed a thick pelt that shaped itself into an arrow before it plunged below his belt.

"I borrowed your razor. Hope you don't mind." Ryerson ran his hand over his jaw, checking for stubble. "I'm a little shaggy in the morning."

"Of course I don't mind," Virginia said quickly. "Here, help yourself to coffee while I use the bathroom."

"Thanks." His attention was not on the coffee, however. He was studying her hair.

"Is something wrong?"

"No." He smiled. "I was just realizing that last night you were wearing a towel wrapped around your head. I never saw your hair."

Virginia put one hand to the chaos of her sleep-tousled, shoulder-length brown hair. "It's a mess. I'd better go do something about it." Hastily she put the cups down on the counter and tried to slip past Ryerson.

But Ryerson made no move to get out of the way. Instead he touched her shoulder as she came to a halt in front of him. The weight of his hand was sensual. Virginia found herself very much aware of it. She stilled uneasily.

Ryerson looked down at her intently, and his fingers moved from her shoulder into the thick tangle of her seal-brown hair. Virginia stared up at him, distantly aware of her own throbbing pulse.

"Thank you for last night, Ginny," Ryerson said softly. "I can't remember the last time I spent such a pleasant evening. The Scotch, the fire, the music and you were just what I needed."

She smiled tremulously and wondered when she had gone from being Virginia Elizabeth to Ginny. It surprised her that the familiar, affectionate form of her name sounded so right coming from him. Something astonishingly intimate had happened out there in front of the fire last night. "It was nothing, really. I'm sorry you had such a long drive on a bad night."

"I'm not." There was a long moment of taut silence between them, and then Ryerson bent his head and found her mouth with his own.

Virginia held her breath, not certain what to expect. She knew she was not a very sensual creature. Her husband had made that clear early in their marriage. But Ryerson was not a flaming romantic, either. He had assured her of that. He probably didn't expect too much from her. And it was after all, just a simple, casual kiss.

The thoughts tumbled chaotically through her head as Ryerson's mouth touched hers and then Virginia relaxed with a small sigh. It seemed the most natural thing in the world to be kissed by this man.

His mouth was hard, warm and subtly demanding. Virginia responded to the kiss instinctively. Nothing had ever felt this right. A. C. Ryerson tasted wonderful, and Virginia realized she had been hungry for a very long time. All her life, in fact.

Her fingertips found his bare shoulder, and she unconsciously flexed her hands, enjoying the feel of strong, smooth muscles under warm skin.

Ryerson groaned softly and raised his head so that his mouth was only an inch from hers. "I think I should tell you something. I've come to the conclusion that I was chasing the wrong sister last night."

Virginia pulled slightly away from him and gazed up into his narrowed silver eyes. She was trembling as if she were on the brink of discovery. The world appeared very new and fresh this morning.

"We hardly know each other," she heard herself say breathlessly and then wanted to scream because of the inanity of the remark. A part of her was convinced she already knew Ryerson very well. How could she not? He was so much like her.

"I would like to get to know you better," Ryerson said, his eyes holding hers. "I think you and I have a lot in common. I do believe, Virginia Elizabeth, that you and I could become very good friends." His fingers tangled briefly in her hair. He was bending his head again to brush his mouth against hers when a key scraped in the lock of the front door. A cold draft of air flowed into the room.

"Ginny! Good grief, it's you, Ryerson! What in the world is going on here?"

Virginia jumped at her sister's startled gasp. Her eyes went to the door behind Ryerson.

"Hello, Debby." Virginia was surprised by the calm in her own voice.

"Well, well, well," Deborah Middlebrook said in a voice that held mingled astonishment and chagrin. "I can't believe it." She came through the door, her slender figure dressed in a chic pair of tight-fitting leather slacks and a huge, glittering T-shirt. Her short blond hair was cut in the latest slightly outrageous style. "What have we here? Finding ways to mend a broken heart, Ryerson? I'm crushed." Her eyes danced. "Positively devastated."

Ryerson turned lazily and examined her with a blandly bored gaze. "I hope you've called your parents. They're worried."

"I'll call them this morning." Debby scanned the tableau of her sister in a robe and Ryerson wearing only his slacks. She shook her head in amazement. "If I hadn't seen it with my own eyes, I wouldn't have believed it. You spent the night here, Ryerson? With my sister? No one in the family is going to believe this. To the best of anyone's knowledge, Ginny hasn't spent the night with a man since her husband died. And she doesn't even know you." The mischief abruptly vanished from Debby's eyes, and her bright gaze suddenly narrowed. "Hey, just what is going on here? Ryerson, if you forced yourself on my sister, so help me, I'll call the cops."

Virginia went a bright pink. Ever since her husband had died, all the Middlebrooks had tended to be a little overprotective. "That's enough, Debby."

Debby glared at her. "No, it's not. Not if Ryerson is playing games." She swung on Ryerson with accusing eyes. "If you're using my sister in some weird way to get back at me, A. C. Ryerson, let me tell you right now, you're in big trouble. My family will be furious. Dad will take you to court."

"Oh, for heaven's sake, Debby," Virginia interrupted swiftly. "Close your mouth long enough to get the facts straight. I don't need you to protect me from Ryerson."

"I'm not so sure about that," Debby shot back. "You may be a few years older than me, but you haven't had any real experience with men, except for what you got out of your marriage, and you sure didn't learn anything useful from that. I'll admit I wouldn't have thought Ryerson was the type to try to seduce you out of revenge, but you never know."

"I assure you," Virginia said with great dignity, "that there is no question of either seduction or revenge involved here. Kindly shut up, Debby."

"Your sister is right," Ryerson said calmly. "Close your mouth, Deb, before you chew off your toes. I give you my word, Ginny and I understand each other perfectly."

"Is that right?" Debby looked skeptical, but faced with two serenely assured faces, she ran out of argument. She glowered at her sister. "When did you give him permission to call you Ginny?"

"I didn't ask permission," Ryerson said before Virginia could reply. "But Ginny doesn't seem to mind, do you, Ginny?" He smiled down at her.

"Uh, no. No, I don't mind at all, *A.C.*"

"Ouch. I guess I had that coming," Ryerson said ruefully.

"Nobody calls him A.C.," Debby said helpfully. She sniffed experimentally. "Is that coffee I smell? I could use a cup."

Virginia's sense of excitement and discovery had evaporated. She wondered if she should be feeling guilty. But one glance at her sister's face told her there was no reason. Debby's wryly amused expression revealed no hint of anguish or despair. Her main reaction, other than amusement, seemed to be concern for her sister's welfare.

Virginia would have been more touched by her sister's attitude if she hadn't long ago told her entire family in no uncertain terms that she did not need or want their protection. She felt quite capable of taking care of herself when it came to men. Of course, she admitted privately, she had not been in any real danger from a man since her husband had died. She had never allowed one to get close enough to hurt her.

"The two of you would probably like to talk," Virginia murmured. "You must have a few details to discuss. Surely the conclusion of an immortal love affair deserves some sort of postmortem. I'll go get dressed." She hurried down the hall to her bedroom.

"I'll show you my broken heart if you'll show me yours, Ryerson," Virginia heard her sister say as Debby sauntered into the kitchen. "But first I need some coffee."

Virginia pulled on the first things she found in her closet—a pair of soft navy wool slacks and a yellow-and-white blouse. Then she brushed her hair into its usual sleek knot at the nape of her neck. When she was finished applying a few light touches of makeup she glanced in the mirror and was relieved to see her normal, serene, decorous, unexciting self staring back at her.

She listened intently for the sound of voices from the kitchen. The conversation between Ryerson and Debby sounded casual and even rather friendly, as far as she could tell. Whatever had ended between her sister and A. C. Ryerson certainly had not warranted the label *grand passion*. Both parties were relieved it was over, just as Ryerson had said.

When she walked back into the kitchen fifteen minutes later, the room was full of the fragrance of scrambled eggs and toast. Ryerson was doing the cooking. He appeared to have made himself at home with her stove and refrigerator. One would think he'd been waking up under her roof for years, Virginia thought. The idea did not bother her nearly as much as it should have. She turned to her sister, who was sitting at the table, sipping coffee. Debby no longer looked worried about Ryerson's presence in the cottage. Her lovely eyes were alight with a familiar mischief.

"Ryerson says he told you about the *big weekend*," Debby said amiably.

"I understand you called off the weekend with your usual flair, Debby. You must have known you'd put Mom and Dad in a tizzy."

"I didn't think they'd see the note," Debby said, wrinkling her pert nose. "It was meant for Ryerson."

"Then you should have made certain it wasn't delivered to my office while your father was there," Ryerson told her bluntly.

"Why did you open it in front of him?" Debby shot back.

"I didn't. My secretary did. She didn't know it was a personal matter. Poor Mrs. Clemens was so astonished that she dropped it. Your father picked it up and handed it to me. But not before he saw your name and glanced at it. He had a right to ask what the hell was going on. I told him."

"Oh, Lord." Debby shook her head. "So that's why you felt obliged to track me down? My parents made a fuss?"

"They were worried about you," Ryerson said.

"Where did you stay last night?" Virginia asked.

"With a friend in Bellevue. But I couldn't stay more than a night with her, and I wanted to be out of touch for a couple of days. I knew Mom and Dad were going to be upset when they found out I was no longer seeing Ryerson. I wanted to give the heat a chance to die down. They've been hoping for wedding bells, you know."

"I know," Virginia said.

"I came here this morning because I thought you would be out of town for a few more days. Hope you don't mind if I hang around a bit."

It was Ryerson who answered. He was dishing up the scrambled eggs. "Virginia might not mind, but I do. You can take off right after breakfast."

Debby glared at him. "Why should I do that?"

"Because I don't want you underfoot while I get to know Ginny," he retorted calmly, carrying the plates over to the table. "It's tough for a man to get over a broken heart when the old girlfriend is making a nuisance of herself. I've got plans and they don't include you."

Virginia's fingers shook slightly as she took her plate. Her gaze leaped to Ryerson's, and she found his silvery eyes smiling at her.

"For pete's sake," Debby complained, "aren't you even going to mourn our lost, dead love for a few days?"

"At my age one doesn't waste time mourning the kind of romance you and I had." Ryerson sat down and poured catsup over his eggs. "As soon as I realized my hearing had not been permanently damaged from heavy-metal music, I was on the road to recovery. Eat your eggs and leave, Deb."

"I've known you for over a month, and I didn't even realize you could cook," Debby grumbled. She dug into her eggs with gusto.

"Which tells us a great deal about our relationship, doesn't it?"

"True. But I think I realized how hopeless our relationship was the night we went to see Sleaze Train and you complained about the music from the minute we left the concert until you dropped me off at my front door."

"Sleaze Train lived up to its name. I've never heard such bad music in my life," Ryerson told her.

"I'm sure you'll enjoy Ginny's taste in music. Strictly retrograde. But don't count on being able to substitute one Middlebrook sister for the other at the altar," Debby advised around a bite of toast. "Ginny made a decision years ago never to marry again. Didn't you, Ginny?"

Virginia raised her brows at her sister. She was not about to let her outrageous sister drag her into this kind of conversation. "I think Ryerson is right, Deb. Why don't you just finish your breakfast and take off?"

Debby widened her eyes in fake shock. "Hey, what is this? A conspiracy to get rid of me? I've been through a traumatic experience."

"You're young," Ryerson informed her dryly. "I'm sure you'll bounce back real quick."

"Oh, yeah? What about you?" Debby retorted.

Ryerson looked across the table and met Virginia's eyes. "Me? I'm going to need plenty of sympathy, consolation and understanding."

"Why do I have this feeling I know exactly where you're going to look for all that sympathy, consolation and understanding?" Debby asked rhetorically. "Ginny, you're not going to let him cry on your shoulder, are you?"

Virginia hid her smile by taking a large bite of fluffy scrambled eggs. "A man who can cook can get just about anything he wants from a woman," she murmured before stopping to think. Her teasing words astounded her more than anyone else at the table.

Ryerson grinned in anticipation. "I'll remember that. Have some more scrambled eggs, Ginny."

"Thank you. Would you please pass the catsup?"

"Lord, how romantic," Debby muttered. "The two of you are going to make a terrific couple. You've got so much in common. People who put catsup on their eggs deserve each other."

Debby left reluctantly an hour later. She complained loudly about having to return to her own apartment where she could count on being hounded by her anxious parents, but her eyes were full of speculative interest as she waved farewell to her sister and Ryerson.

Virginia watched her sister guide the little sports car out of the sodden driveway and then she turned to Ryerson. A slow, satisfied smile edged his mouth.

"Two of a kind," he said softly, sounding pleased. "How do you feel about that, Virginia Elizabeth?"

She thought about it, aware of a distant, beckoning promise of happiness. She did not trust the lure, but she could not bring herself to resist it. She took refuge in practicality. "It's a little soon to know, isn't it?"

"No, it's not too soon to know. Not for me. But I'm willing to give you plenty of time." He stroked one blunt finger along the edge of her jaw. "We don't have to rush into anything. We're two adults who can take our time."

She touched his hand, taking pleasure in the strength in it. "Yes," she agreed. "We can take our time." She could get her feet wet very slowly, and she would not have to wade too deep. Ryerson was the kind of man who would let her run back to shore if she chose.

"I told you I'd like to get to know you much better, but in a way I already feel I know you very well." Ryerson's fingertip moved down the column of her throat to the curve of her shoulder. "You said last night that you would be interested in a friendship with a man."

"I would like that," she said quietly and meant it. She could see herself becoming very good friends with A. C. Ryerson. And perhaps, just perhaps, the association might blossom into something more than a friendship. She knew she was not cut out for a Grand Passion, but for the first time since her husband had died she found herself considering the possibility of a warm, comfortable, safe relationship that would prove satisfactory to both parties.

She halted her thoughts as she realized how far ahead they were spinning. There was plenty of time to see where it all led. It was enough for now just to feel that she was on the same wavelength as Ryerson. In fact, it was the most delightful sensation she had ever had with a man. She wanted to treasure it fully and understand and explore it completely.

"We'll take it slow and easy," Ryerson promised again. "No rush. I think you and I will become very close friends, Ginny."

Friends. Virginia smiled very brilliantly. "That sounds wonderful."

'No rush." The reassuring words echoed again and again in Virginia's mind during the next three weeks. She would find herself pausing for a few minutes at her desk to think about them. They would float through her consciousness just before she went to sleep. She would repeat them to herself in the shower.

"No rush." She had found a man who was content to let a relationship build slowly, easily, naturally into a close friendship before he made any demands on her; a man who was willing to give her time. She and Ryerson would become good friends before they decided whether to take the risk of going to bed together. The knowledge was infinitely reassuring to Virginia.

For the first time since her disastrous marriage, Virginia could accept the fact that she might really be able to establish a close relationship with a man. And if she chose the right man, an understanding, undemanding man, she just might be able to perform adequately in bed. Ryerson wouldn't expect fireworks.

Almost four weeks after she had found Ryerson on her doorstep, Virginia met her sister for lunch at a downtown café. Debby showed up with several shopping bags. She was her usual eye-catching self in a sizzling red short skirt and a matching bolero jacket. She examined Virginia's tailored business suit and sleek hair and frowned slightly but said nothing. She was accustomed to her sister's more conservative ways.

"All right, let's have it," Debby demanded as soon as they were seated. "How's the big love affair going? We all know you and Ryerson have been seeing each other constantly for nearly a month. Mom and Dad are afraid to get their hopes up again, but personally I'm feeling very positive about the future. I think you and Ryerson are meant for each other."

"That's very generous of you," Virginia said blandly. She opened her menu and studied the list of pastas. The dish with olives, capers and basil looked especially interesting. Her appetite seemed to have increased a little lately. Usually she just had yogurt or a salad for lunch. "But just to set the record straight, there is no flaming love affair. Ryerson and I are friends."

Debby peered at her over the top of the menu. "Come on, Ginny, don't be coy. This is me, Debby, your nosy sister. What's going on between the two of you?"

"Well, last Saturday Ryerson and I spent a wonderful evening at the ballet," Virginia said sedately. "On Tuesday we had dinner on the waterfront. Excellent Alaskan salmon, by the way. I think we're going to attend a program of chamber music in the university district this weekend. We haven't quite decided on that, though. Also, there's a new exhibit of cacti at the conservatory in Volunteer Park that we've been meaning to tour."

Debby raised her eyes toward the ceiling. "An exhibit of cacti. Heaven help us. That's not what I meant and you know it. I want to know if you're sleeping with the man, darn it!"

It was Virginia's turn to raise her eyebrows. "You always come directly to the point, don't you, Deb?"

"Sure. Most folks think it's part of my charm. Now level with me, sister dear."

Virginia smiled loftily. "Your question does not deserve an answer, but I'll give you one, anyway, mostly because I know it will drive you nuts. I am not sleeping with him. Furthermore, I'm not at all worried about it one way or the other. Ryerson and I have already decided we have all the time in the world. We're not going to rush into anything. We're more concerned with becoming good friends than we are with being lovers."

"Hmm." Debby tapped the white tablecloth with one long, mauve nail. "Ryerson is a nice guy but I've seen the way he looks at you, Ginny. I'll tell you something. He never looked at me that way. He's got more than friendship on his mind. Does he know about your marriage?"

"He knows I was married once, yes. So was he. It was a long time ago for both of us. We don't talk about it."

"I mean, does he know just how bad things were for you during those three years you were married?" Debby persisted.

Virginia's smile vanished. "Not even you know just how bad things were, Deb."

Debby had the grace to blush. "I've seen the way you've avoided any real entanglements since Jack's death. It doesn't take a genius to figure out just how scarred you were. Your family is bound to be very interested in the fact that you've finally started getting serious about someone. We're all hoping for the best, but we're a little nervous, too."

Virginia sighed. "I know. Everyone's feeling quite protective. It's touching in a way, but totally unnecessary. Ryerson and I understand each other. We're going to take our time."

"Is that his chief asset as far as you're concerned?" Debby asked shrewdly. "He's not the type to rush you?"

"It's certainly a relief to find a man who is content to take things slowly," Virginia admitted.

Ryerson was so tender, so considerate, so kind and so content to let her set the pace of the relationship, Virginia reflected happily. A woman could count herself very lucky indeed to have a friend such as A. C. Ryerson.

'No rush."

Ryerson listened to his own words as they echoed mockingly through his head and wondered if he had been temporarily insane when he had given Virginia the glib promise of plenty of time.

He had been dating her for a full month now, and he was starting to climb the walls. It was ridiculous. It didn't help to remember that he'd dated Debby for a full month and barely noticed the lack of sex in the relationship. Things were vastly different this time around: he was definitely noticing the lack with Virginia Elizabeth. He hadn't felt this constantly aroused, constantly frustrated, sensation since high school. The unrelieved desire was becoming downright painful.

Ryerson got up from his desk and stalked to the window to glare down at the panorama of functional, utilitarian buildings and yards spread out around the offices of Middlebrook Power Systems. The southern end of Seattle was given over to manufacturing, shipping and industrial plants of various sizes and kinds. Generally speaking, this part of town was not the home of high-tech research, accounting firms or stock brokerage houses. This was the muscular side of Seattle, and the grime showed.

But there was money to be made here, as Boeing had proved over the years. Middlebrook Power Systems had always been profitable. Ryerson intended to make it even more so. He was content to have the company headquartered here in the heart of hardworking Seattle. The honest surroundings suited the product. Things were on track in his business life, Ryerson reflected.

The problem in his private life, he decided, bracing one hand against the windowsill as he gazed out over the landscape, was that it was Ginny's nature to proceed slowly and cautiously. He could hardly blame her. He was, after all, a lot like her. And truthfully, he had to admit a month was nothing in the overall time frame of a relationship. In three months he might have legitimate grounds to start wondering if things were headed in a sensible direction, but he certainly shouldn't be getting this anxious after only four weeks.

But he wanted her. Badly. The knowledge flared within him, an undeniable, unrelenting fact that he had to deal with on a daily basis.

Some primitive part of him was awake and prowling restlessly, yet Ginny seemed content to let matters drift in the uncertain territory of male-female friendship. Ryerson didn't doubt that she was expecting the same conclusion he was anticipating, but he was definitely doubting his own ability to last until it all came together for them.

She was enjoying the time they spent with each other, Ryerson told himself. He was certain of that. And he was seeing to it that they spent as many evenings as possible together, though ferry schedules were becoming a damned nuisance.

He was also certain of the extent of her response to his kisses. She went into his arms more and more willingly each time he reached for her, and she trembled sweetly when he touched her breasts. He found the response endearing. Her lips parted eagerly when he silently asked for surrender, but he sensed the lack of expertise in her kisses and wondered at it. She seemed warm and willing but strangely unsure of herself.

Inevitably she always found a gentle, firm way of ending things before they progressed to bed. And Ryerson, trapped by his own promise, had been reluctant to press her very hard.

Ryerson's fingers tightened around the wooden sill, and he felt a cold chill. He was never going to last. He had no way of knowing how long Ginny wanted to spend enjoying the preliminaries, but he suspected she would be content to go on like this for quite a while. She didn't seem in the least anxious to move toward bed.

He would be a basket case within another month.

What he needed was a way of breaking the platonic pattern that was forming in their relationship. Things were too serene, too calm, too sedate, too easy for Ginny to manage. Maybe a trip would be the answer. New and romantic surroundings as well as the sense of being outside the normal routine of life might encourage her to view their friendship in a new light.

Ryerson nodded to himself and walked back to the desk to pick up the phone and call a travel agent.

* * *

Virginia was enjoying the view of Elliott Bay from Ryerson's downtown condominium and eating a marvelous grilled salmon that he had cooked himself when the plane tickets appeared. She was so startled when Ryerson put them down on the table in front of her that she nearly dropped her fork. Her eyes flew to his.

"Are you going somewhere on business?" she asked.

He looked at her, silver-gray eyes intent. "No. We're going somewhere. For pleasure, not business. I want to take you away for a few days. I think we need some time alone together. You mentioned you had some vacation time. Will you come with me, Ginny?"

She went still, sensing that something was about to change in their relationship and not at all sure she was ready for the change. "Where?"

"A little island in the Caribbean off the coast of Mexico. It's called Toralina. I've got reservations at a first-class resort. It's right on the beach. Brand-new. Features dancing every night under the stars, a casino, gourmet food and endless sand. With any luck the sand and the food will be separate. What do you say? Can you get a few days off?"

Virginia swallowed, a wave of uncertainty washing through her. She wasn't ready for this. Only a week ago she had been bragging to Debby about how she and Ryerson were going to take their time developing a close friendship.

But Virginia knew that if she accepted this offer of a trip to Toralina, she was tacitly accepting a radical change in her relationship with Ryerson. She was no fool. She knew that Ryerson was using the trip as a way of asking for a more physical commitment. If she went with him, he would expect her to share a hotel room. He would expect her to sleep with him.

He had been kind enough to suggest an excuse, if she felt she needed one, Virginia realized. He had asked her if she could get the time off. All she had to do was say no. She knew he would understand that she was not yet ready.

But when would she be ready, Virginia asked herself silently. How long was she planning to take before she went to bed with Ryerson? A few more weeks? Months? She didn't know the answer to that question.

The plane ticket in front of her was Ryerson's way of asking her that same question. Maybe it was time they both discovered the answer. She considered Ryerson her best friend in the whole world, but if she couldn't give him what he needed in bed it would be better for all concerned if they faced that now rather than later.

"I'd love to go with you to Toralina," Virginia said softly and wondered at her own daring.

THREE

She was far more nervous than any normal bride would be on her wedding night. But then, Virginia knew better than most brides how devastating a wedding night could be. She had to remind herself that this was most definitely not a wedding night. It was just the first night with Ryerson.

She would not panic, she promised herself.

Nevertheless, another chilling tremor of uncertainty went through Virginia as she dressed with painstaking care for dinner. Words such as *bride* and *wedding night* had a way of doing that to her. Some people panicked at the thought of spiders or airplanes. She panicked at the thought of marriage.

Deliberately she pushed the feeling aside. The last thing she needed to do was start rehashing the memories of her all-too-real wedding night and the nightmare of a marriage that had followed.

She was perfectly safe, Virginia reminded herself for the thousandth time. After all, she wasn't marrying

Ryerson; she was merely attempting to start an affair with him. And Ryerson was nothing like her dead husband. Ryerson was her friend, her companion, a man with whom she had everything in common.

Virginia had been repeating the litany to herself since the evening Ryerson had put the tickets to Toralina down in front of her and asked her to go with him to the island. Amid the flurry of packing and getting ready for the trip, she had done a good job of convincing herself that everything was going to be all right. But tonight a lot of suppressed anxiety was surfacing. The evening was balmy and warm, but Virginia felt little chills down her spine and her palms were alternately hot and cold.

She was not marrying the man. She was only going to attempt to go to bed with him. Ryerson wasn't the sort to expect too much from her.

Or was he?

He was, after all, a disturbingly virile man. She might not be the passion queen of the century, but that didn't mean all her female instincts were blunted. She was perfectly capable of sensing the strong vein of controlled sexuality that ran beneath the surface in Ryerson. It was why she had agreed to this trip. Virginia had known that sooner or later the sexual issue had to be settled between them. Both of them had to learn the truth about this side of their friendship.

She finished zipping up the flower-splashed yellow silk she had bought especially for the trip to Toralina. The full skirts of the gown drifted weightlessly around her ankles. The wide sleeves were caught in deep cuffs that emphasized her elegantly shaped hands. The neckline was discreet, displaying a hint of throat and shoulder but no cleavage. Debby had argued for a dress that did more to showcase her sister's magnificent bosom, but Virginia knew she would never have been comfortable in it. She wasn't the sort to wear low-cut dresses.

She wore her hair down tonight. It fell in a smooth, heavy curve on either side of her face, just brushing her shoulders.

Virginia slipped on her high heels and walked over to the window to examine once again the dreamlike view. Beyond the gardens outside the luxurious suite an endless vista of turquoise water and sky stretched to the horizon. A wide strip of sand marked the beautiful beach below. Hillsides that were lush with tropical vegetation embraced the resort. The elegant hotel was a picturesque cluster of brilliant white walls and red-tiled roofs. The place didn't look at all like Seattle, Virginia thought in amusement. It was a fantasy setting. And that was a good thing.

It was a perfect place to begin a full-fledged affair, and there was no doubt but that Ryerson had brought her here with that purpose in mind.

What she needed, Virginia decided as she turned away from the window, was a drink. A large one.

She crossed the wicker-furnished bedroom, ignoring the wide bed that dominated it and opened the door into the sitting area. She took a deep breath as Ryerson put down the *Wall Street Journal* he had been reading and got to his feet. For a moment she simply stared at him, distantly aware of a sense of longing.

He looked so good, Virginia thought wistfully. The kind of man who had the calm self-assurance it took to look terrific in the conservative black-and-white evening clothes he was wearing.

"I think that must be the original power suit," Virginia said lightly. "You look fabulous."

Ryerson searched her face for a few seconds, and then he smiled slowly. "You're the one who looks fabulous tonight." He came toward her, his eyes drinking in the sight of her. "Very exotic and a little mysterious."

"I don't feel quite like myself tonight," she admitted.

"Neither do I. I haven't given more than two minutes' thought to diesel engines since we got here." Ryerson's silver eyes gleamed. "Maybe the tropics are good for us, Ginny. Maybe this is just what both of us needed." He slid one large hand under the bell of her hair and cupped her nape. Then he bent his head and kissed the curve of her throat.

Virginia closed her eyes and yielded momentarily to the small shiver of anticipation that went through her. It was going to be all right, she told herself. When she lifted her lashes again, Ryerson was looking down at her with an expression that was both infinitely possessive and infinitely tender. She gathered her courage to ask the question that was seething within her.

"Ryerson," she whispered, "I have to ask you something. Something important."

He nodded patiently. "Anything."

"Will you…that is, if things don't…don't quite work out tonight. I mean, if it's all a big mistake and everything goes wrong will you still want to be my friend?"

"*Ginny.*" He groaned as he dropped a feather-light kiss on her nose. "What's the matter with you, honey? Nothing's going to go wrong. We're friends and we're going to become lovers. What could possibly go wrong?"

"But if it doesn't work out. If we don't become lovers, will we still be friends?" She had to know, she told herself.

Ryerson's eyes met hers in a steady, reassuring glance. "You're really nervous about this, aren't you?"

"A little." And that was the understatement of the century.

"Honey, we've been friends since that first night. Nothing's going to change that. What's going to happen between us in bed will only deepen our friendship. Now what do you say we take these two people who happen to be good friends out for an evening in paradise?" His large hand closed around hers, his eyes asking for much more than a dinner date.

Virginia retreated from the issue that was worrying her so much and took refuge in humor. "You're not even talking like a man who's very big in diesel motors."

He trailed a finger across her bare shoulder. "We're even. You're not dressed like a lady who's made a career in information storage and retrieval."

Virginia grimaced. "Don't remind me. Do you think the dress is a bit much?"

"I think the dress is perfect."

They stepped outside into the warm, fragrant evening and walked along a secluded, flower-lined path. The main building of the resort was located some distance away, hidden by the thick greenery that provided privacy for the individual suites. The hotel gardens were virtually a tropical forest—heavy, lush and wild. As they walked, Virginia occasionally caught sight of other guests who were also making their way toward the resort's core.

"I thought we'd have drinks on the terrace and then go in to dinner. The casino opens at nine," Ryerson said.

Virginia slanted him a curious glance. "Do you gamble?"

"Rarely. I play poker once in a while but that's about it. This trip is the biggest gamble I've taken in years. How about you?"

She went pink at the obvious meaning in his words. "Same here," she admitted dryly.

Ryerson grinned and tugged her a little closer to his side. "Think of me as a sure thing."

If only she could guarantee him the same in return, Virginia thought fleetingly.

The terrace bar was already crowded by the time they arrived. They found a small table in a secluded corner, and Virginia ordered a large margarita instead of her usual white wine. Ryerson stuck to Scotch.

Some of Virginia's nervousness slipped away as the tequila took hold. Conversation with Ryerson, which had been a bit stilted prior to the drink, resumed its normal easy flow. The island felt like another world.

By the time they went into the open-air dining room to feast on conch chowder, crisp, fried plantains and fish poached in lime juice, Virginia was feeling a little better. She was a million miles away from Seattle and her own past. The bottle of wine Ryerson ordered with the meal added to the effect.

"I'm feeling lucky tonight," Ryerson announced after dinner. "Let's try the casino."

He took Virginia's hand in his and led her into the glittering casino where tuxedoed croupiers dealt cards and rows of silver slot machines tinkled merrily.

The room was full of fashionably dressed hotel guests. The atmosphere could not have been more removed from reality. Virginia's feeling of having stepped into a different world intensified. She watched Ryerson play blackjack for a while, and then she tried her hand at the slots. Ten dollars worth of tokens tumbled into her hands the first time she pulled the handle. She added them to Ryerson's blackjack winnings.

"You were right," she told him with a laugh. "This is our lucky night." When a hostess came by with a complimentary glass of champagne, Virginia helped herself. She couldn't bear to have the marvelous sense of unreality begin to fade.

But as she tipped the flute to her lips, Ryerson gently captured her wrist. He looked down at her with a half-amused, half-concerned expression.

"Careful," he advised. "It's easy to lose track when you're enjoying yourself the way you seem to be tonight."

She frowned slightly. "Lose track? Oh, you mean the champagne. Don't worry, Ryerson. I'm feeling great. Never felt better, in fact. I promise not to pass out on you."

"I'm not so sure about that." Deftly he removed the glass from her hand. When she started to protest he laid a finger against her lips. "Trust me. You're not used to this kind of wild living. Don't overdo it or you'll pay for it all day tomorrow, and that would be a shame. We don't have forever here. Only a few days. I don't want us to waste a single one."

He didn't understand, Virginia thought resentfully. She didn't care how bad she felt tomorrow as long as she got through tonight without disgracing herself. "I'm not worried about tomorrow. Why should you be?" she asked.

"Not worried about tomorrow?" Ryerson mocked. "Come now, that doesn't sound like my Virginia Elizabeth."

"Maybe I don't want to feel like Virginia Elizabeth tonight," she retorted.

"Who do you want to feel like?"

She blinked at the question. "I'd like to be the woman you want me to be tonight."

The laughter faded from his gaze and the silvery eyes. "The woman I want you to be is the woman you are, Ginny. You don't have to become someone else."

"That's what you think," she muttered. Then she brightened, determined not to lose the ground she had already gained. "Let's go watch the poker players for a while."

Ryerson said nothing, but he allowed her to lead him over to a roped-off dais where several men in evening dress sat playing poker. One of the players, a young, redheaded man in his late twenties, seemed more intense than the others. Smoke drifted upward from the cigarette in his fingers. He was winning heavily.

As Virginia and Ryerson watched, the players dropped out one by one until the redheaded man was left with the pot. As he collected his winnings, he glanced up, and Virginia was startled by a pair of feverishly bright blue eyes. The man was obviously high on his victory. As Ryerson started to turn away with Virginia in tow, the stranger spoke.

"Hey, there, you with the lady in yellow. Can I interest you in a game? You look like a man with a sense of adventure."

Ryerson glanced back over his shoulder and shook his head politely. "Not tonight, thanks. Maybe some other time."

"Anytime, but why not tonight? The name's Brigman, by the way. Harry Brigman. I'm riding a streak of luck that just won't quit."

"So am I," Ryerson said with a small smile. He squeezed Virginia's hand. "So am I."

"Well, why don't we get together with a few of these other gentlemen and see what happens?" Brigman said cheerfully.

Virginia felt Ryerson hesitate. She looked up at him. "If you want to play for a while, go ahead. I don't mind."

He considered the matter. "You know, the funny thing is, I do feel lucky tonight."

"Then go ahead and play." Virginia knew she was deliberately buying a little more time for herself, but she ignored the fact. "I'll watch."

Brigman gazed at them speculatively. "Maybe the lady's your good-luck charm, friend."

"Maybe she is," Ryerson agreed casually. He looked down at Virginia, his decision appearing suddenly in his eyes. He brushed her mouth with his own. Then he stepped up onto the dais and took a seat at the card table. He glanced back once to make sure Virginia was nearby.

She rested her elbows on the polished wooden rail that surrounded the playing area and smiled reassuringly. A poker game could last for hours, she reminded herself. Plenty of time for her to work up a little more courage.

She was right about one thing—the poker game went on for some time. As soon as it started, Ryerson, along with every other man at the table, quickly forgot about her. Virginia watched the game for a while, but most of the subtleties were lost on her. She knew next to nothing about poker. After a while she wandered off to get another drink at the bar.

When she returned, there was no sign of any letup in the intensity of play. Ryerson had his jacket off, as did most of the other men at the table, but that was the only concession made to the tension. Virginia did notice that the pile of chips in front of Ryerson seemed to be growing. She took that as a good sign.

She leaned against the railing again, drink in hand, and admired Ryerson's calm, unruffled technique. Nothing seemed to faze him. He could have been doing paperwork in his office for all the emotion he displayed. Brigman, on the other hand, appeared to be getting more and more tense and agitated. It was obvious he was starting to lose, and the experience appeared to be new to him. He did not care for it.

Another hour passed. Virginia wandered away to listen to the band. Two men asked her to dance, but she politely declined. When she returned, she realized the poker game had reached a crisis of some kind. Everyone seemed to have dropped out except for Ryerson and Brigman. There was sweat on Brigman's brow. It trickled down his nose. He wiped it off with an angry, impatient hand before saying something in a low voice.

He spread his cards on the table, and Ryerson did the same. From where she stood, Virginia could not see the hands and wouldn't have been able to decipher them if she had, but she knew a loser's face when she saw it. Harry Brigman had just lost badly. He got to his feet with a jerky movement and murmured something to Ryerson. Then he turned and strode out of the casino. Ryerson rose more slowly, stretching his shoulders. He glanced around and saw Virginia.

"I'll be back in a few minutes," he said quietly.

"Where are you going?"

"Brigman and I are going to talk privately. Stay where you are." Without waiting for her reply, he followed Brigman out of the casino.

Virginia waited impatiently, curious and somewhat alarmed. She wondered what had happened during the game that required a private consultation between Ryerson and Brigman. She was about to follow the two men out of the casino when Ryerson unexpectedly returned. Brigman was not with him.

"What in the world is going on?" Virginia demanded softly as she hurried to meet Ryerson.

Ryerson's eyes were glittering. A tightly leashed excitement radiated from him. "Brigman just covered his losses, that's all."

"But how? Why did you have to leave? What's happening?"

"Hush. I'll tell you all about it. Let's get out of here."

He took her arm and led her out into the balmy night. When they were safely out of sight, he drew her to a halt near a garden light and reached into his jacket pocket. "Take a look at this."

Virginia studied the small jewelry box in his hand. It was old, covered in green velvet. A strange sense of exhilaration gripped her. "What is it?"

Without a word Ryerson opened the box and exposed the contents. Virginia caught her breath. For a second she could not move. Her gaze was riveted on what lay inside the velvet container.

It was a bracelet. An incredible bracelet. Unlike any bracelet Virginia had ever seen. Green flames frozen forever in clear stones shimmered in the soft light. Gold linked the individual emerald fires to small diamonds. The whole piece glowed with a warmth that was surely unnatural for a cold piece of jewelry.

Virginia could not find words as her sense of reality shifted slightly. Tension seized her. For a timeless moment she had the disconcerting feeling that she was looking at an object that was not bound completely to the same dimension in which everything else around her existed. The object in the box seemed to be simultaneously part of the past, the present and the future.

An unfamiliar sense of possessiveness leaped into life within Virginia. *The object in the jewelry box belonged to her and Ryerson.* She knew that with a deep, absolute certainty.

Virginia shook off the unsettling sensations that had taken over her emotions. She finally found her tongue.

"It's a bracelet."

"Emeralds and diamonds linked with gold," Ryerson said. "Or so Brigman claims."

"Do you believe him?"

"I'm not sure. I'm no jeweler."

"It's stunning, Ryerson. Absolutely beautiful. Even if it's a fake, it's the most fascinating piece of jewelry I've ever seen."

"If it's a fake, it's a very good one. Look, here's a formal jeweler's appraisal of the age of the bracelet." Ryerson indicated a folded piece of paper lying under the velvet cushion. "It doesn't indicate the value but it does claim the thing is late seventeenth century."

"Incredible."

Ryerson closed the box, his gaze very brilliant. "I felt the same way when I saw it," he said roughly. "The minute Brigman opened the box and showed it to me,

I knew I had to have it. I told him I'd accept it as full payment for what he lost to me tonight."

"Did he lose that heavily?"

"When the game ended, he owed me over ten thousand dollars."

Virginia's mouth fell open. "Ten thousand dollars?" she squeaked. "Ryerson, you gambled for that kind of money?"

"I told you I was feeling lucky." His brief grin was wicked.

"Yes, but *ten thousand dollars*? I can't believe it. What if this bracelet is a fake? Unless those stones are real, it won't be worth anything near ten thousand."

Ryerson dropped the box back into his pocket. "And if the stones are real, it's probably worth a lot more than ten thousand. Brigman didn't have any choice. He didn't have ten grand on him. This was the only thing he could use to cover the debt. One way or another, I have the feeling I've got my money's worth." He smiled at her with satisfaction. "Come on, Virginia Elizabeth, let's go have a drink. I could use one."

"So could I," she agreed weakly. She felt dizzy and not just from the drinks she'd already had. The idea of a ten-thousand-dollar poker game was enough to make anyone light-headed. "It's so unlike you," she murmured wonderingly.

"What?"

"Playing for those stakes."

Ryerson grinned again, looking arrogantly triumphant. "Lady, the evening is young, and I'm still feeling lucky. This is my night."

She wasn't sure how to take that remark, so she let it slide. Besides, she was beginning to feel some of Ryerson's triumph. She had never seen anything in her life as beautiful as the emerald-and-diamond bracelet.

"Maybe I really am your lucky charm," she murmured daringly.

"I never doubted that for a minute," he assured her.

For the first time, Virginia began to look forward to the end of the evening.

They danced until shortly after one o'clock, and Virginia was amazed by the small but definite sense of anticipation within her. Instead of the anxiety that had been gnawing at her all day, she was now filled with a delicate excitement that was completely unfamiliar.

Maybe everything really would be all right tonight. Maybe her friendship with Ryerson could be extended to include a successful affair with him. She nestled closer to him on the dance floor, and Ryerson's arms tightened around her. She was aware of the hard edge of the bracelet box inside his jacket. And that was not the only hardness she felt when Ryerson held her this close, Virginia realized.

She and Ryerson were in the middle of a slow, sensuous number when the decisive moment arrived. She had been cradled contentedly in his arms, her head on his broad shoulder and her eyes almost closed when he spoke softly in her ear.

"Let's go back to the room, honey. It's way past our bedtime. I think it's time to see just how lucky I'm going to get tonight."

The gentle, unreal feeling of happy anticipation that she had been enjoying wavered slightly. Virginia tried to cling to it as she stirred and lifted her head. With a twinge of anxiety, she realized she was not quite ready. She made a small show of glancing at the watch on her wrist.

"It's just one o'clock. The night is still young by jet-setter standards," she pointed out with a false cheerfulness.

"I'm sure the rest of the jet-setters will excuse us," Ryerson murmured, taking her arm to guide her off the dance floor.

Maybe another drink would help, Virginia thought. "How about a nightcap under the stars?" she suggested brightly.

He looked down at her, silver eyes silently questioning. "All right, if that's what you want."

She nodded quickly. "I'm sure that's the sort of thing real international jet-setters do."

"Far be it from me to spoil the image."

Ryerson took her to the terrace bar and sat her down in a wicker chair. He ordered two brandies and then settled back to sip his.

"It's beautiful, isn't it?" Virginia said, taking a too-large swallow of the brandy. Her throat burned, and she barely stifled a cough.

"The sea is fine. But you're the most beautiful thing on the horizon," Ryerson said quietly.

Virginia's head snapped around, and she found him watching her with eyes that were the same color as the silvery sea. There was no element of teasing or flirtation in his gaze. Ryerson wanted her, and his need was starkly evident in his face. Virginia raised the brandy snifter to her lips.

But Ryerson reached out and stayed her hand. "Does it really take another dose of alcohol to make going to bed with me seem like an interesting thing to do? I'm your friend, Virginia, remember? You can tell me the truth. If you don't want to go to bed with me, just say it."

Instantly Virginia was swamped with despair. None of this was his fault. She struggled for a weakly reassuring smile. "I guess I'm a little nervous."

He answered her smile with a faint curve of his hard mouth. But his eyes were full of understanding. "If it's any consolation, so am I. Under the circumstances, I don't think that's so strange. This is beginning to feel like the first night of a honeymoon, isn't it?"

Virginia stiffened and then forced herself to relax. It was not the first night of a honeymoon, she reminded herself. Ryerson hadn't really meant that. Just a poor choice of words. "You're nervous, too?"

"Yeah."

For some reason she found that vastly comforting. "We have a lot in common, don't we?" she asked wistfully. "Right down to getting nervous about something like this."

"I think we'll both be fine once we get started," Ryerson said gently. His eyes were bottomless pools of silvery moonlight.

Virginia moistened her dry lips. It was going to be easier knowing Ryerson was a little uncertain, too. She tossed down the rest of the brandy with a flourish. The time for action had arrived.

"Well, if you think we'll both do all right once we get started, then by all means let's get started. Let's get the whole thing over and done with and see what happens," she said with brisk determination. She shot to her feet and imperiously held out her hand to Ryerson. "You're right. It's time to go for it. No pain, no gain. Onward and upward. I'm ready if you are."

Ryerson eyed her summoning fingers for a few seconds and then looked up at her with a strange expression. "This isn't the Charge of the Light Brigade, you know. If you'd rather wait . . ."

"No, absolutely not. Never put off until tomorrow what should be done tonight," she declared in ringing tones. Her decision was made. It had been made from the moment she had accepted the ticket to Toralina. Her courage was as high as it would ever be. "It's now or never. No more waiting. You invited me on this trip for a specific reason and I came along knowing that reason. I'm sick of being a coward. It's time we both found out the truth once and for all." She grabbed his hand and tugged him to his feet.

"The truth about what?" Ryerson asked as she pulled forcibly on his hand. He allowed himself to be drawn slowly to his feet.

"Never mind," Virginia said as she swept him out the door and down the stone path that led to their suite. "The main thing is to keep the momentum going. Ride the wave. Go with the flow. Mustn't get cold feet now. It's do or die. Now or never."

"I was wrong. This does seem to be turning into the Charge of the Light Brigade, after all," Ryerson observed warily as he obediently let himself be dragged down the path. "I can't help wondering why. Is there something we should talk about first, sweetheart? Are there cannons out there in the valley that I don't know about?"

"This isn't a time for talk; it's a time for action," she told him stoutly.

"If you say so. But, Ginny, there's no need to rush into this. You said yourself it's still early. We've got all night."

She came to a sudden halt and whirled to face him. "This was all your idea. Have you changed your mind?"

Ryerson barely avoided colliding with her. He stared down into her fierce expression. "No, honey, I haven't changed my mind. But I'll admit I don't understand your attitude."

"There's nothing to understand," she told him aggressively. "I'm ready. You're ready. Let's go do it."

"Right," he agreed blandly. "I won't argue with that logic." He took the key out of his pocket and inserted it in the lock. When he stood politely aside, Virginia sailed into the room, pulling him after her.

As soon as she had him over the threshold, she slammed the door and locked it. Then she swung around to confront him. She was trembling with something that might have been excitement or terror. In that moment she honestly did not know which emotion was causing her pulse to race.

With her eyes never leaving Ryerson's intent gaze, she quickly unbuttoned the wide cuffs of the yellow silk gown. Ryerson said nothing. He just watched with an unreadable expression as she reached behind herself and fumbled with the zipper.

She lost a little nerve as the bodice started to crumple to her waist. Hastily she caught the soft fabric in both hands and held it over her full breasts.

"Want some help?" Ryerson asked with grave politeness.

Virginia shook her head quickly. "No. No, I'm fine. Excuse me, please." She rushed into the bedroom and flung the door closed behind her. Frantically she hunted through the closet for the new nightgown she had purchased for the trip. It was in there somewhere. She distinctly remembered unpacking the thing. Clutching the dress to her breasts, she bent over to see if the nightgown had somehow slipped to the floor of the closet. Behind her the door opened.

Virginia gave a small gasp of alarm and stood up so quickly that she hit her head on the closet doorknob.

"Damn!" She groaned and rubbed the injured spot. The silk dress fell to her hips, revealing her prim cotton bra and the waistband of her equally demure white cotton panties. Belatedly Virginia grabbed the bodice of her gown.

"Are you all right?" Ryerson came slowly into the room, loosening his tie. He had already discarded his jacket. He was carrying the jeweler's box.

"I'm fine," she assured him breathlessly.

"Ginny, are you sure nothing's wrong?" Ryerson slung the tie down over a chair arm.

"Of course there's nothing wrong. What could be wrong? This is a very straightforward situation, isn't it? I mean, you and I here together. We're just good friends who are going to...to go to bed together. A very friendly thing to do. It was bound to happen sometime, wasn't it?"

He came closer, unfastening the buttons of his white shirt. "Yes, it was bound to happen sometime." He looked down into her wide, anxious eyes. "I've been wanting you since the first night I met you."

She swallowed. "You're absolutely sure of that?"

His eyes narrowed thoughtfully as he studied her tense face. "Absolutely certain. But it's no good unless you feel the same way. Do you want me, Ginny?"

"Yes," she gasped. "Yes, I want you." It was true, she realized with an inner start. For the first time she acknowledged to herself that she really did want him. She wasn't doing this just to please him; she actually wanted to go to bed with Ryerson. But wanting him and being able to satisfy him were two entirely different things.

"Then I don't see any problem."

"Lucky you," she murmured under her breath.

"Honey, it's me. Your friend. Remember?" His shirt fell open. Ginny stared at the broad expanse of his chest.

"None of my friends have ever looked like you," she heard herself say in a faint voice. Her eyes followed the trail of dark, curling hair down his flat stomach to where it disappeared beneath his belt. The strong, ag-

gressive outline of his body below the belt was ample
proof of her statement. Most definitely none of her
friends looked like him. Ryerson was a big man, and he
would have big appetites. She had to satisfy him. She
just had to. She couldn't bear it if she failed tonight as
she had failed with her husband.

"Ginny, honey, I promise you that none of my friends
have ever looked like you, either. None of them have
ever turned me on the way you do."

"Oh, Ryerson." She gave a small cry and without
pausing to think she released the bodice of her dress and
flung herself into his arms.

Ryerson chuckled softly, sounding relieved and very
pleased. He wrapped her close against him. "It's going
to be okay," he said into her hair. "Everything's going
to be all right."

Opening the jewelry box behind her back, he removed the bracelet and carefully fastened it on her
wrist. He tossed the empty box down on the dresser and
studied the glittering stones on her arm.

"It was made for you," Ryerson said softly.

Virginia looked down at the bracelet and knew
somehow that he was right. It had been made for her
to wear. With Ryerson.

The bracelet felt unexpectedly warm on her wrist.
Virginia was surprised. She had thought it would feel
cool to the touch. "You want me to wear it? Now? In
bed?" she asked uncertainly.

"Does that seem a little too kinky to you?"

"No, no, not at all. A bit exotic, perhaps, but not really kinky. It's just that I've never worn anything like this to bed before."

"We're even. I've never been to bed with a woman who was wearing emeralds and diamonds," Ryerson interrupted gently. "Tonight is going to be very special for both of us." He touched her shoulder lightly, his fingertips a little rough against her soft skin.

Virginia clutched him around the waist. Everything would be all right as long as she kept going forward and didn't lose her nerve, she thought. Ryerson felt good. Warm and heavy and right. Just as the bracelet did on her wrist. Her nerves seemed to be humming with genuine excitement now, not fear. For the first time she allowed herself real hope. She was beginning to think she might be able to get through this, after all.

The important thing was not to lose her nerve.

Under no circumstances must she give herself a chance to lose her nerve. *Forward*.

Driven by a sense of urgency, Virginia reached up to push Ryerson's shirt off his shoulders, and then she quickly fumbled with the zipper of his trousers. She had his pants halfway off when she remembered his shoes. Things were already getting awkward, she thought uneasily as she knelt at his feet and struggled with his shoelaces. Ryerson reached down and tangled his hands in her hair. She sensed the sexual tension in his touch. It sent a ripple of response through her.

Ryerson patiently allowed her to undress him down to his briefs, his expression half-amused and totally aroused as he watched her. When she was finished, she stepped back with a small frown to see if she had over-looked something. Not that anything about Ryerson was easy to overlook. He was very large and very male standing there in front of her, wearing only his briefs. Virginia chewed on her lower lip.

"Hey, it's me," Ryerson said softly. He stepped forward and tilted her face up so that she was forced to meet the desire in his eyes.

"Let me undress you now," he said thickly. He tugged her gently into his arms.

Virginia could feel the unmistakable hardness of his body as he pinned her close. He was hard all over, she thought in vague wonder. His shoulders, his thighs, his smoothly muscled back all seemed strong and tight and hard. She inhaled the earthy scent of him and realized she found it tantalizing. Something unfamiliar vibrated within her.

Then she felt his hands on the silk dress, pushing it carefully down over her hips. It fell to the floor near his trousers and shirt and Virginia was now violently aware of her near nakedness. She searched Ryerson's face anxiously for any sign of disappointment.

"You're beautiful," he said in a voice that was dark and vibrant with his desire. "You're all a man could want." His hands drifted down over her full breasts. He unclasped her plain, functional bra, dropped it on the floor and took the weight of her into his warm palms. His thumbs moved slowly over her nipples. Virginia shivered and closed her eyes for a moment. His hands felt so good on her body.

Before she had completely adjusted to the feel of his touch on her breasts, Ryerson's strong, sensitive hands slid downward to settle on the curve of her hips. He flexed his fingers on her buttocks and groaned. Then, as if unable to help himself, he lowered his head and kissed her deeply.

Reassured that nothing had gone wrong yet, Virginia resumed her rush toward bed. She gave herself no chance to respond to Ryerson's kiss. There was no need to dawdle over that part, she told herself. She already knew he liked kissing her. The worst was still ahead of her, and she wanted to get it over with so that the truth would be out at last.

Pulling free of his arms, Virginia turned and dashed over to the closet. She yanked on the nightgown, which, mercifully, was quickly located on the closet floor. The garment was new, but it looked very much like all the rest of her lingerie. It was made of plain, practical cotton, long sleeved with a prim neckline.

Using the soft material as a screen, she wriggled out of her panties. Then she scooted over to the bed and ripped back the covers. She bounced down onto the mattress, grabbed the sheet to her breasts and pasted on what she hoped was a welcoming smile.

"Maybe you should have had a little more brandy," Ryerson observed ruefully as he walked slowly over to the bed.

"Come to bed, Ryerson. Let's not waste any more time."

"If you're sure this is the way you want it," he muttered, "who am I to complain? I sure as hell am ready.

And there will be time enough later to take it slowly. I want you so much, sweet Ginny."

He stripped off his briefs, revealing the hard, thrusting reality of his manhood. Virginia sucked in her breath, and her sense of resolve wavered again. Ryerson was definitely built to scale.

She was no lightweight herself, Virginia thought bravely. Theoretically she and Ryerson should fit very well together.

Before she could give herself any more pep talks, Ryerson was beside her on the bed, putting a hefty dent in the mattress as he reached for her. She was trembling when she went stiffly into his arms, but she was more determined than ever to finish what she had started.

When her arm went around his shoulders, moonlight glanced off the emeralds on her wrist. Virginia saw the gleaming flash and felt oddly reassured. She was doing the right thing, she told herself.

Ryerson loomed over her, all massive shoulders and lean, hard muscle. She felt one of his legs snag hers, and a tiny frisson of panic escaped in spite of her determination to contain it. She squelched it at once.

This was Ryerson, she told herself over and over again. It was going to be all right. Dear heaven, it had to be all right. She wouldn't be able to bear it if he wasn't satisfied with her.

Ryerson ducked his head to kiss her breast, and Virginia held her breath. She thought she liked the feel of his tongue on her nipple, but she couldn't concentrate on the delicious sensation it caused. She was too busy worrying about what came next. When his hand moved down her side to her thigh, she tensed.

"Ginny?"

"Yes, Ryerson?" She clutched at him, her nails digging into his shoulders.

"This is going to work a lot better if you relax."

"I can't relax," she wailed. "I told you, I'm a little nervous. How do you expect me to relax?"

"I might have been right earlier when I said this was like the start of a honeymoon. This is beginning to feel like a wedding night, all right. A Victorian wedding night. What are you planning to do? Lie back and think of England?"

Virginia froze. If he got impatient or lost his temper she wouldn't stand a chance of pulling this off. "There's no need to get angry. I'm doing my best." Her voice was barely audible.

Ryerson made an impatient movement and cupped her face between his hands. His expression revealed concern as well as desire. "You're not making me angry. I'm just trying to figure out what the hell is going on here."

"We're supposed to be making love," she reminded him through gritted teeth. "Why don't you get on with it?"

He stared down at her from suddenly narrowed eyes. "I will," he finally said. "But I think I'll do it my way, not yours."

Virginia wanted to scream. "What's wrong with the woman taking the lead?" she challenged in an unnaturally shrill voice. "I thought men liked to get it over with fast."

He shook his head, smiling faintly. "Believe me, I have no objections to your taking the lead. But first you're going to have to catch up with me."

"What do you mean, catch up with you?" she asked in utter bewilderment. "*Ryerson*, what are you doing?"

"I'm going to give you a small head start."

He caught both her hands in one of his and gently held them together above her head.

"Wait. Ryerson, what's going on?" Her voice was a soft shriek of genuine alarm.

"Sorry, sweetheart, but at the rate you were going, you were about to draw blood."

She closed her eyes in humiliation as she realized just how deeply she had been digging her nails into his shoulders. The poor man must have been suffering terribly. "I'm sorry," she got out.

"Don't be sorry," he said as he carefully parted her legs with his free hand and inserted his knee between her thighs. "There's a time and a place for everything. We'll get to the point where I won't mind having your nails in my back. But first we need to cover a little more territory."

"I don't understand."

"I'm beginning to realize that. Just relax, sweetheart, and pretend you're involved in an information retrieval search on your office computer."

"A search!" A small, despairing laugh was forced out of her.

"That's better," Ryerson said approvingly. Continuing to anchor her wrists above her head, he bent down to kiss her again.

He took his time, inviting her to remember the kisses they had shared in the past. She had enjoyed those kisses, knowing they were safe, knowing he would not demand more of her than she could give.

Virginia gave a tremulous little sigh. She knew and loved Ryerson's kisses. She could enjoy them without fear. Slowly she gave herself up to the familiar caress and parted her lips willingly when his tongue stole into her mouth.

For a long time he made no further demands. It was as if he were perfectly content to go on kissing her all night long. Virginia moaned softly and ceased thinking about the immediate future. Her senses began to swim with pleasurable anticipation. A deep restlessness started to uncoil within her.

"That's it, sweetheart. That's my beautiful, sexy Ginny. Honey, you don't know what you do to me. You feel so good. I've been wanting to have you like this for weeks."

He kept talking to her in that soft, rough, warm voice. She heard the words of encouragement and reassurance, but what really registered was the tone of them. Ryerson's voice was dark and thick with passion. He told her over and over again how much he wanted her and described in graphic detail exactly what he was going to do to her. To her utter astonishment, Virginia found herself responding to the promise of passion in his words.

It was unlike anything she had ever known. Hesitantly at first, she allowed herself to explore the sensations pouring through her.

At first she simply floated. Ryerson's hands continued to move on her, and something hot and demanding stirred to life within her. Slowly she let herself be tugged deeper into a mysterious whirlpool. She twisted against Ryerson, unconsciously seeking more of him.

"That's it, Ginny. That's the way I want you to feel." His hand slipped down over her stomach to the soft nest below. Virginia started to return to reality with a rush. She knew what came next. She was prepared for it. She tensed again and opened her eyes as she struggled to free her hands.

Ryerson held her still, soothing her carefully. "I'm just going to touch you. It's all I want to do right now."

"It's not all you want," she retorted achingly. "I'm not stupid. And I want what you want, Ryerson. I want you to make love to me. I'm ready now."

He trailed a finger into the warm dampness between her legs. Virginia shuddered in startled reaction. "You're a lot readier than you were a few minutes ago," he agreed in satisfaction. "But you still haven't caught up with me. You wanted to take the lead, remember?"

"Yes, but . . ."

"Hush, love." He kissed her back into silence. "We really do have all night. I swear to you that all I want to do at the moment is touch you."

Virginia searched his silver eyes and decided he was telling the truth. There was nothing to worry about yet. He was just going to touch her. She relaxed once more

and made no move to resist when Ryerson opened her
legs a little wider.

Ryerson began to tease her with his hands, probing
gently, coaxing forth a response. Virginia gasped. She
had never experienced such erotic sensations. Instinctively she began to move, urging him to explore her
more intimately, frustrated when he continued to tease
and tantalize.

She tried to free her hands again, not because she
wanted to push him away but because she needed to
persuade him to carry out the intimate promises he was
making.

Ryerson loosed her wrists and groaned apprecia-
tively when she instantly grasped his hand and held it
more tightly to her.

"Oh, yes, baby," he muttered. "Show me what you
want. Show me exactly how hard and how deep you
want it."

Virginia could no longer contain the unfamiliar sensation that was pouring through her. She arched against
Ryerson's hand once more, feeling his fingers go deep
inside her. She cried out and clutched Ryerson.

He came to her then, moving quickly on top of her
and sheathing himself tightly within her just as the full
force of her climax gripped her.

Virginia cried out again as her body sought to adjust
to the masculine invasion. But she gloried in the tight,
hard feel of him within her and another amazing wave
of release went through her. She clung to Ryerson,
wrapping her legs around him and whispering his name

over and over again as he thrust deeply into her softness.

Then Ryerson went rigid. He shouted her name in a
strangled gasp as he surged into her one last time. He
held on to her as the storm washed through his body,
and then they were both tumbling into warm oblivion.

Moonlight drifted through the window, seeking emeralds and diamonds and gold. Flames flickered within
crystal-green stones. The bracelet seemed warmer than
ever on Virginia's arm.

FOUR

Ryerson awoke at the first hint of the Caribbean dawn.
He lay quietly for a few minutes, conscious of the
warm, soft, womanly weight on the bed beside him and
of the spectacular clarity of the pale light outside the
window.

He realized he had never felt better in his whole life.

Briefly he entertained the fantasy that he and Ginny
were alone on a distant planet, the only two human
beings on a fresh, young world waiting to be popu-
lated.

Ryerson decided he could really get into the concept
of populating planets with cute little Virginia Eliza-
beths and some little Angus Cedrics. The job would
require a lot of effort and dedication on his part, of
course. He would probably have to spend most of his
time in bed with Ginny, but a man did what he had to
do. Populating planets was important work.

Virginia shifted slightly beside him, and the sunlight
danced on the bracelet on her wrist. She had forgotten

to take it off before going to sleep, he realized. Idly he eased the sheet down to her waist, enjoying the view of wildly tousled hair, full breasts and gently rounded arms. He smiled with possessive satisfaction. Ginny was glorious in her nudity, his very own lush, pagan goddess. The glitter of the bracelet added to the impression. He was getting hard just looking at her.

Ryerson let his mind drift back over the events of the night. Nothing had ever been this right. Last night had been the most deeply satisfying night he had ever spent in his life. But then, he'd never gone to bed with such a good friend before, he reminded himself with a small, triumphant grin.

There had never been anyone like Ginny for him. Soft and generous and passionate, yet filled with a womanly strength that was ideal for his own size and strength. He remembered her initial anxiety and wondered at it again. How could she have doubted herself? Or was it him she had doubted? Some of Ryerson's arrogant satisfaction faded slightly at the thought. He wondered if she had been hesitant about going to bed with him because she was afraid he wouldn't live up to the standards set by her dead husband.

Ryerson forced himself to relax again as he recalled the way Virginia had eventually responded to him. She might have been nervous and skittish at first, but in the end she had given herself completely to him. Ryerson wondered how his fierce and growing possessiveness fitted in with Virginia's definition of friendship.

More memories of the night floated into his head. Hot, sensual memories that triggered hot, sensual reactions in his body. Ryerson recalled the way Virginia's legs had circled his driving hips and the way she had clung to him as her release washed over her. Her eyes had widened first in shock and then closed in ecstasy. Remembering her silent astonishment the first time she had surrendered to the demands of her own body, Ryerson again questioned just what had gone on in her marriage. Maybe her dead husband's standards hadn't been so high, after all. Maybe her dead husband had been a jerk.

Ryerson glanced down at where the sheet covered his lower body and grinned to himself. Too much early-morning fantasizing. It was time for this particular Adam to wake his Eve.

He turned on his side, intending to kiss Ginny into wakefulness, but something stopped him. Ryerson found himself studying her intently, instead. It was the first time he had awakened beside her, and he wanted to savor the moment.

She looked simultaneously innocent and sensual in the morning light. She was lying on her side, her back toward him. Her thick brown hair was fanned out on the pillow, and her long lashes hid her clear hazel eyes. The sheet foamed below her ripe breasts and flowed over the enticingly full curve of her hips. He had been right about one thing, Ryerson reminded himself. Virginia Elizabeth had some sexy, solid shape to her.

And she'd had the damnedest effect on him, he thought ruefully. Never before had he felt compelled to pin any woman down and make love to her until she shivered helplessly in his arms. It was a side of himself that he'd never experienced. He'd never been so desperate to have a woman respond to him before, either.

Virginia stirred again, one long leg shifting under the sheet. Ryerson propped himself on his elbow, ran his fingertips across the stones in the magnificent bracelet and then leaned over and dropped a warm kiss on her bare shoulder.

"Wake up, woman; we have work to do."

Virginia twisted luxuriously, letting herself come slowly to wakefulness. A small smile played around her lips as she realized where she was and who was with her. The morning sun was just beginning to stream through the open window, bringing with it the scent of exotic flowers and a mysterious sea.

Last night the waves had been crashing on the beach, she remembered. Last night, she had been caught in those breakers, swept out on the crest of a gem-green sea and tossed up onto a golden shore. It had been a glorious, exciting, intensely erotic experience. She was involved at last in the kind of affair she had never dreamed existed in reality, at least not for a woman such as herself. She opened one eye and surveyed Ryerson's face.

"Work?" She yawned. "What work? We're on vacation."

"That's what you think. We have a whole planet to populate." He closed a hand over one breast, teasing the nipple with a gentle scraping action of his palm.

Virginia opened both eyes and stared at him. "We *what?*"

"Don't panic. We can handle it. If we get busy."

She blinked. "You're losing me, Ryerson."

"Not a chance. Now that I've finally got hold of you, I have no intention of letting you slip away."

Virginia saw the warmth in his eyes and blushed in spite of herself. "What's all this about populating a planet?"

"Just a harmless morning fantasy. I had to fill the time somehow while I waited for your majesty to awaken. Look out that window. Doesn't it seem as if we're the only people in the world?"

Virginia glanced out at the fresh dawn. "Mmm. I see what you mean." She covered his questing hand with her own, her eyes searching as she gazed up at him. "It does seem as if we've stepped into another world. I don't feel at all like myself this morning. This is going to be a very special week, isn't it, Ryerson?"

His hand slipped out from under hers, tugging the sheet a little farther down over her hips. "Very special." His thumb grazed over a budding nipple, and he watched with satisfaction as the nipple went taut. "What do you mean, you don't feel at all like yourself?"

She hesitated, thinking of the joys of the night that had been hers. "Let's just say I don't feel like an information storage and retrieval manager this morning."

"And I've hardly given a thought to diesel engines or power systems since I woke up. But that doesn't answer my question."

Virginia sensed the direction of his probing and tried to deflect it. She put on what she hoped was a deliberately inviting smile and began to toy with the crisp, curling hair of his chest. Her eyes dropped meaningfully to where the sheet covered his lean hips. "I don't think this is the time for questions. It looks like you've got more urgent problems."

Ryerson grinned wickedly. "You learn fast. What makes you think you can use sex to distract me?"

She widened her eyes in mocking innocence. "I don't know what gave me the idea. It just sort up sprang up out of nowhere. Will it work?"

He gave the matter a moment's close thought. "Maybe. Temporarily. If you really work at it."

She tossed back the sheet and rose on her elbow. "I'm a very hard worker," she promised. Then she pushed experimentally and Ryerson obediently went over onto his back. He lay looking up at her with anticipation, silver eyes full of sensual challenge.

Virginia responded to the look in his eyes out of the newfound self-confidence she had gained during the night. She knew now that Ryerson would react satisfactorily to her touch, and the knowledge filled her with the kind of pleasure and power only a woman can know.

She touched him with daring intimacy, gliding her fingers down his chest to his thighs. There she found him hard and heavy and waiting. She caressed him delicately until Ryerson groaned and started to reach for her. Evading his grasp, she boldly bent her head and tasted him with exquisite care the way he had tasted her during the night.

Ryerson sucked in his breath. "Oh, Ginny, you don't know what you're doing."

"No? What am I doing?"

"Playing with fire." He pulled her down astride him, guiding her legs around his hips. She braced herself on her knees and looked down at him, enjoying the position. He gave her a smile that said he knew exactly how she was feeling. Then he began to stroke her, playing with all the dark, secret places that quickly grew warm and moist at his touch. When she arched her neck and sighed, he deepened the touch.

"*Ryerson.*" She reached down and cupped him gently.

"A little closer, sweetheart." He cradled her hips in his hands and began to ease her onto his manhood. "That's it." He probed her carefully and began to fill her with himself. "That feels so good, so damned good. I think you must have been specially built just for me. Definitely one of a kind."

Virginia delighted in his muffled groan of desire, feeling him sink deeply into her softness. Then she began to move slowly, aware of his fingers continuing to tease her even as she set the pace.

The thrilling release blossomed quickly, swamping both of them for a few timeless moments. Virginia collapsed languidly on Ryerson's chest and sighed in contentment. Nothing in her life had ever been this good or this satisfying. Nothing had ever made her so aware of her fundamental femininity. For the first time she was learning that she could, indeed, please a man and take her own pleasure in return.

In that moment she decided she was content to be friends for life with A. C. Ryerson.

She was given little chance to enjoy the afterglow. Ryerson recovered all too quickly. He slapped her lightly on her bare bottom and eased her down onto the bed. Rising to his feet, he stretched magnificently.

"Let's hit the showers. I'm starving and breakfast is waiting."

Virginia blinked. "Are you always this perky in the mornings?"

He cocked one brow. "Perky? I don't know about perky, but I am definitely hungry in the mornings. Usually it's just for food, but this morning it was for you and food. Now that I've had you . . ." He let the sentence trail off meaningfully.

"Now that you've had me, you're ready for the food," Virginia concluded ruefully. "Nice to know your priorities in life."

He leaned over her, caging her briefly between his hands. His grin was all-male. "Hey, you were at the top of the list, weren't you? Stop complaining. If you're very sweet, I might let you come into the shower with me."

Virginia batted her lashes at him. "The thrill of a lifetime, I'm sure."

He laughed and scooped her up in his arms. "Judge for yourself," he told her with lofty arrogance as he carried her into the bathroom.

Virginia, who hadn't been carried in a man's arms since she was a small child, was too startled by the position in which she found herself to argue.

A short time later she conceded that showering with Ryerson was definitely a thrill.

But the early-morning sensual romp did not deflect Ryerson's questions. She knew she had only bought a little time. When he led Virginia down onto the beach for a walk after breakfast, she was resigned to the inevitable. She supposed it was only fair that really close friends shared this kind of information about each other. Mentally she prepared herself.

"I'd like to know," Ryerson said deliberately as he clasped her hand in his, "what was going on in your mind last night when you were working so hard to get up enough nerve to go to bed with me."

Virginia winced. "It wasn't like that. Not exactly."

"It was exactly like that."

"I told you, I was a little anxious. It had been a . . . a long time, and I guess I felt a bit awkward."

"It was more than that, Ginny." He glanced down at her, his eyes thoughtful. "You were scared to death. Once you'd made the big decision, you just wanted to get it over with as quickly as possible. What did you think was going to go wrong?"

She kicked sand with her bare feet and stared out to sea. He had a right to know, she decided. After all, she had behaved in what must have seemed a very peculiar fashion for a woman of her age and experience. "It's a little hard to explain."

"Was it me? Were you afraid I wasn't going to live up to expectations?" he asked roughly.

Ginny was shocked. "It wasn't anything like that!"

"So talk to me, Ginny. I'm a good listener."

She smiled in spite of herself. "Yes, you are. Well, if you must know, I was scared to death of going to bed with you."

"I got that feeling," he said wryly. "But why, Ginny?"

"You think of me as a confident, mature woman, but in that one area of my life, I'm not at all sure of myself. At least, I wasn't until last night." She turned her head and looked up at him, her eyes narrowed against the bright morning sun. "I want you to know how happy you made me last night, Ryerson."

He released her hand and put his arm possessively around her shoulders. "In case you haven't realized it, the feeling was mutual."

She took a deep breath. "I'm glad."

"It has to do with your marriage, doesn't it?" he asked when she didn't volunteer any more information.

"My nervousness?"

"It was much more than nervousness. I was nervous myself. What you were feeling was more on the level of outright panic. It took a hell of a lot of courage for you to go through with it. Why?"

"I guess there's no need to drag this out any further," she said, willing herself to get it all said. "It's obvious you won't be satisfied until you've heard all the gory details. To put it simply, my marriage was a terrible mistake. And I was naive enough to believe it was all my fault."

"What made you think that?"

Her mouth twisted grimly. "I'd better start at the beginning. Jack worked for my father. He was a rising star in management. Everyone approved of him, and when he started courting me, they all approved of the marriage. I was rather dazzled by him, I admit. He was good-looking, charming and charismatic. But on some level I felt I didn't really know him. I ignored that, though, because everyone liked him."

"In other words, you didn't quite trust your own judgment in the matter, so you relied on everyone else's judgment?"

She smiled wryly at his perceptiveness. "Not entirely. I really did think I was in love. I would never have married him otherwise. Jack was a dynamic, fascinating man. But things started going sour on our wedding night. My husband managed to perform his, uh, husbandly duties, but it was obviously not the supreme moment of his life. And it was a crushing disappointment for me. Nothing like knowing you've failed to satisfy your husband to make a woman start married life feeling like a total failure. Jack had a lot of subtle techniques for ensuring I assumed all the responsibility for that failure. He was good at that kind of thing, I eventually discovered. A real con man. Manipulative and clever. He had a real talent for controlling people."

"So you managed to marry a real bastard first time out of the gate." Ryerson's arm tightened comfortingly around her shoulders. "It happens."

"I suppose so. But I never dreamed it would happen to me. Jack made it clear I was not his ideal woman. He let me know I was too big, too, uh, full figured for his taste. He preferred dainty, petite types. I floundered badly for months, trying to figure out what I was doing wrong and wondering why he had married me in the first place. Like a fool, I kept making compromises, giving ground, deferring to him, trying to please and placate him. I had a mental image of what a good wife should be, and I kept trying to live up to that image. But nothing worked. The truth didn't dawn on me for some time, however."

"What was the truth?"

Virginia shook her head grimly. "I finally came to my senses and realized that Jack had married me because he hoped Dad would eventually turn over Middlebrook Power Systems to his new son-in-law."

"Ah, the picture becomes clear. Why didn't you file for divorce and get the hell out of that situation, Ginny?" Ryerson gave her a small, admonishing shake.

"It took me months to figure out that the only way out was divorce. For some idiotic reason I kept trying to patch up the marriage. I felt I had to try. Everyone kept saying how great Jack was. What a perfect husband for me. What an asset he was to Dad's firm. But in the end, I gave up. I found a lawyer and started divorce proceedings. When I informed Jack I was leaving he was furious. He threatened to ruin my father if I went ahead with the divorce."

"How the hell did he manage a threat like that?"

"Jack had become very powerful at Middlebrook. On the pretext of taking a load off Dad's shoulders, he had assumed a great deal of control. I knew him well enough by then to believe he might actually be able to hurt the firm. I felt trapped."

"Did you talk to your father? Tell him what was going on?"

"I was afraid Dad wouldn't believe me. He and everyone else were really mesmerized by Jack. They trusted him completely. Everyone did. I had to agree to stay in the marriage until I could figure a way out. I could not bring myself to share a bedroom with him, but that was just fine with Jack. He had made it clear he was bored with me in bed, anyway. I nearly went crazy trying to find a way out of that terrible situation. I felt absolutely desperate. Talk about stress. I nearly collapsed from it. I had finally decided I had to talk to Dad when I got the news that Jack had died in a car accident. I know it's an awful thing to say, but frankly, I have never been so relieved in my life as I was the night the hospital emergency room phoned to tell me Jack had been brought in DOA. I was suddenly free."

"You did a two-year sentence in hell, and you've decided never to risk the trap of marriage again."

Virginia took a deep breath. Ryerson was the first person who had ever really understood what it had been like. "The irony of the whole thing was that when it was all over, my father confided that he'd begun to have serious doubts about Jack, but he hadn't wanted to say anything to me."

"Ah, my poor Ginny. No wonder you've never been tempted to remarry. You got nothing out of that relationship except the feeling you were a failure as a woman."

"I guess that sums it up. A real disaster."

Ryerson came to a halt and turned to take her face between his large hands. His eyes burned into hers. "Virginia Elizabeth, how could you ever have doubted yourself that way?"

She clung to his wrists. "I made up my mind after Jack died that I would never marry. Marriage holds nothing for me. For me it will always symbolize being trapped. But there were times when I longed for a companion and a friend."

"Never a lover?"

"I was afraid to want a lover," she said honestly. "I was convinced I could never really satisfy a man. When you showed up on my doorstep I knew you could be my friend and companion, but I didn't know what I would do when you tried to become my lover. I also knew that sooner or later that bridge would have to be crossed."

"But you kept trying to postpone sex?"

"I knew I couldn't keep postponing it indefinitely. You were very tolerant but I knew you were getting restless. When you bought those tickets, I understood what you were asking, and I knew I had to face the inevitable. I tried to tell myself that if I worked very hard at it and if your expectations weren't too terribly high, I just might be able to get through it without turning you off completely."

Ryerson shook his head in exasperation. "With an attitude like that, it was no wonder you felt obliged to down a few margaritas, half a bottle of wine and a glass of brandy before you did your duty. What a little idiot you were," he added fondly. "The idea is to enjoy yourself, not twist yourself into a nervous wreck."

"Enjoying myself was the last thing I was worried about," Virginia admitted. "I wasn't even thinking about that end of things. But I was petrified that you would find me less than satisfactory. I didn't know how I was going to deal with that. I told myself that you were a lot like me, that you were my friend, that you wouldn't expect fireworks. But I was so scared I wouldn't even be able to create a small blaze."

Ryerson grinned slowly. "You're wrong. I did expect fireworks. Every time I kissed you, I could feel the fuse being lit. I knew damned well that when the time finally came, we were going to cause an explosion."

Virginia went pink. "Well, I'm glad you had so much faith in me, because I certainly didn't."

He pulled her close, pushing her head tenderly against his shoulder. "Did you enjoy the fireworks when you finally discovered them, sweetheart?"

She sensed the masculine satisfaction in him and chuckled. Lifting her face, she smiled into his eyes. "You know perfectly well I did. I suppose you're going to take full credit?"

He laughed deeply. "I'm willing to let you have some of the credit. You're the sexiest thing I've ever encountered in or out of bed." He kissed her thoroughly, and his hold on her tightened. The laughter went out of him, to be replaced by a more intense emotion. "Ginny, I can't remember the last time I felt anywhere near this sure of things. We're going to be so good together."

Virginia relaxed into his embrace. The affair was well and truly launched. She had found a man who was right for her at last. Her good friend had become her lover.

The emerald-and-diamond bracelet on her wrist flashed in the sunlight.

That afternoon Virginia browsed through the resort boutique and found a new dress that appealed to her. Her sister would have approved instantly. It wasn't at all the sort of dress Virginia would normally have glanced at twice, and she wasn't sure what made her so determined to buy it. It was made of light, gauzy emerald-colored cotton and had a series of flounces around the hemline that were edged in gold ribbon. It had a multicolored sash. But its most interesting feature was the low neckline.

It was far more daringly cut than the yellow silk she had worn the previous evening. In fact, it was more daringly cut than anything she had ever owned. But a sense of adventure was compelling her, and before she gave herself time to consider too carefully, Virginia bought the dress.

When she emerged from the bedroom that evening, Ryerson looked up expectantly. His expression altered almost comically when he saw the new addition to Virginia's wardrobe. His face revealed a variety of expressions ranging from mild shock to a severe frown. Somewhere in between was a flash of what looked like pure lust.

"Like it?" Virginia twirled around to display the whole effect. "It's a perfect dancing dress. And the bracelet goes perfectly with it, don't you think?"

"I like what there is of it," he retorted dryly as he came forward to take her arm. "But for pete's sake, don't slouch or drop anything tonight."

"Why should I worry about that?"

"Because if you have to bend down, the top half of that dress is going to fall off."

Virginia grinned. "It only looks as if it might fall off. It's actually quite well engineered."

Ryerson arched his brows skeptically and drew a finger slowly along the line of her décolletage. When Virginia trembled delightfully in reaction, he smiled knowingly. "It's my business to know good engineering when I see it, honey, and I can tell you right now, this dress is as shaky as a bridge made out of toothpicks. Remember what I said about minding your posture."

"I'll remember," she promised demurely as she straightened her shoulders. She smiled a secret smile as they went out the door.

Ryerson glanced down at her, a cryptic smile of his own edging his mouth. "Fireworks can be a lot of fun, Ginny. But you have to be careful when you play with them."

"Why?"

"Because you might get your fingers singed."

Her eyes were alight with mischief as she slid him a sidelong glance. "I'll be very careful."

"Why do I have trouble believing that?"

The evening air was heavy with the fragrance of flowers. The dying sun left a residual warmth in the stones of the path that wound through the gardens to the main building of the resort. Virginia could feel the heat through the thin soles of her delicate high-heeled sandals. She was about to comment on it when a familiar figure stepped out of a neighboring suite directly into their path. His back was toward them.

"Hello, Brigman," Ryerson said easily.

The redheaded man spun around, looking startled. Then he relaxed and gave them a rather forced smile. His eyes darted to the bracelet on Virginia's wrist and then flicked back to Ryerson. "Evening. Heading for dinner?"

"Thought we'd have a drink first," Ryerson responded.

"Good idea. I'm heading in the same direction. Mind if I join you?"

Ryerson hesitated, and Virginia knew he was trying to think of a good reason to refuse the casual request. Apparently nothing came to mind, because he finally nodded brusquely. "Sure. Why not?"

"Thanks. I see you're enjoying your winnings," he added with another glance at Virginia's wrist. His smooth gambler's voice almost succeeded in concealing the underlying tension that radiated from him. "I'll have to admit that emeralds and diamonds do something for a woman. When are you going to give me a chance to get my bracelet back, Ryerson?"

Virginia instinctively moved the bracelet out of sight behind a fold of her dress as Ryerson said something bland and noncommittal. Virginia glanced at Brigman. "Do you play poker regularly?"

Brigman shrugged modestly. "It's how I make my living."

Virginia was startled. "You make your living at cards?"

He smiled thinly. "What can I say? I'm good at it, and I manage to earn enough to be able to afford to live in hotels like this one." He waved a hand to indicate the elegant resort. "It's a good life. Never gets boring, I'll say that for it. The one thing I can't take is being bored. There are a lot of places like Toralina with easygoing gambling laws. Around here they don't mind if a few of the guests get into a private game and set their own stakes. I'll be honest with you, I don't generally lose." He glanced at Ryerson. "You surprised me last night. I would never have pegged you for a pro."

"I'm not. I surprised myself," Ryerson said coolly. "I told you, I felt lucky."

Brigman's eyes narrowed speculatively. He did not appear convinced. "Well, my offer is open. If you feel like trying your luck again, let me know. I expect to earn enough tonight at the table to stake myself to another game with you. I'd like to get that bracelet back."

"Thanks for the offer," Ryerson said. "I'll think about it."

"You do that. I don't mind telling you that bracelet was pretty special to me. Old family heirloom, you know. Came down to me from my grandmother. It's been my good-luck charm for years."

"I see." Ryerson's tone was still noncommittal.

Virginia was relieved when Brigman took himself off to a far corner of the bar. She touched the bracelet to reassure herself it was safe. "I don't like him," she said as Ryerson found a private table. "He's too slick. Reminds me of Jack, in a way. You're not really going to let him talk you into another game, are you? Not with the bracelet at stake?"

"Relax. I've lost all interest in poker. Last night was the first time I've really felt like playing in years, but the urge is gone now. I have no intention of gambling away that bracelet. It belongs to you and me. I think I'm beginning to see it as a symbol of some sort."

"A symbol of what?"

Ryerson looked at her across the table, his gaze serious. "I'm not sure. Maybe a symbol of what we found together in bed last night. Emeralds and diamonds and gold go nicely with passion, don't you think?"

Virginia's eyes were glowing with happiness as she leaned forward to touch his hand. "I think they go beautifully together."

Instead of answering her glowing look with one of his own, Ryerson frowned abruptly. "Sit up straight, Ginny. You're going to fall out of that dress."

"I had no idea you had such a prudish side to your nature," she remarked as she straightened obediently.

"Any woman who buys the kind of prim, plain white cotton underwear you collect has no grounds for calling anyone else prudish," he retorted.

Virginia blinked uncertainly, wondering if he really had found her underwear terribly unexciting, and then she saw the teasing glint in his eyes. She relaxed. "Well, you'll be happy to know I've learned my lesson. Take a good look down the front of this dress, Ryerson. I'm definitely not wearing my Sears bra tonight."

"So I see." He eyed the roundness that was exposed by the daring neckline. "I take back what I said about prudishness. What are you wearing under that dress?"

"Nothing at all," she returned blithely. "I told you the dress was beautifully engineered." She propped her elbows on the table, folded her hands and leaned her chin on them. The net result was to enhance the cleavage. "I feel different tonight, Ryerson. What about you?"

He made a production out of having to force his gaze back to her face. When he saw that her eyes were serious, he bit back the outrageous remark he had been about to make and said instead, "I know what you mean. I feel different, too."

"Maybe it's part of the transformation."

"What transformation?"

She shrugged. "The sense we both have of being in a different world down here. I think we're both feeling more adventurous or something."

"Or something," he agreed dryly. "Be careful when you move your shoulders like that."

"Wouldn't it be strange if this were the real us?" Virginia went on whimsically. "Maybe we were born to be a pair of exotic adventurers, cruising from island to island."

Ryerson's mouth curved faintly in amusement. "And how were we born to support ourselves while we cruise exotically?"

Virginia thought about that. "I don't know. You seem very good at poker. Apparently there's a living to be made from that sort of work. Brigman's surviving by playing cards here in the islands."

Ryerson laughed. "Don't get your hopes up. I'm a fair poker player, but that's about it. I was feeling lucky last night, and I took a chance. Normally I would never have risked a game with a professional like Brigman. I'm still not sure what made me do it. But last night I was on a roll. I got lucky in more ways than one last night." He paused to leer cheerfully. "I'll tell you one thing, we wouldn't get very far on my poker-playing talent if we had to rely on it for a living. I'll stick to diesel engines."

Virginia's eyes flirted outrageously with him. "I have great faith in your talents, Ryerson. I'm sure you could make a living playing cards if you really tried."

"Oh, yeah? What happens the first time I lose?"

"I'll think of a suitable consolation prize," she promised softly as she hunched her shoulders slightly and leaned forward again.

"I'm going to have two very suitable consolation prizes in my hands in another minute if you don't sit up straight."

Virginia's smile became even more brilliant.

Ryerson groaned and ordered his Scotch in a low growl that made the cocktail waitress jump.

He was under a spell, Ryerson decided later that evening. It was the only explanation. He'd had some experience with sex and some experience with friendship, but he'd never had any experience with the kind of magic he was sharing with Virginia. He felt as if he were getting tangled up in a glistening, shimmering web.

The magic was changing him in some indefinable ways, he discovered. It was releasing some very old instincts, for one thing. He couldn't remember the last time he had felt so territorial, for example. The precarious cut of Virginia's dress was never far from his mind. He found himself glaring at other males frequently.

It was totally out of character for him to tell a woman what to wear and what not to wear, but by midnight he had decided he was not going to allow Virginia out in public again in her new dress. Not that the thing didn't look fantastic on her. But she was too tall and too magnificently proportioned to go unnoticed when she was attired the way she was this evening. It seemed to Ryerson that every man on the dance floor had sneaked a peak at the woman in his arms.

One man in particular was edging closer. Ryerson noticed him first when he was sitting at the bar. He was nearly as tall as Ryerson, which made him just the right size for Virginia. That fact alone was enough to irritate Ryerson. But there were some additional, equally annoying facts.

The stranger had the kind of looks Ryerson knew women usually admired. The guy was built along lean, slender lines with light brown hair, a mustache and a pair of dark eyes. He appeared to be a couple of years younger than Ryerson, and he was dressed in white slacks and a blue blazer. It was the kind of outfit that belonged on board a large, gleaming yacht. Ryerson's newly aroused territorial instincts sent up several warning signals when the man turned again to gaze at Virginia.

"Ouch! You're squashing me," Virginia complained as Ryerson gathered her closer.

"I'm trying to cover the gap in that dress."

She looked up at him with bewitching eyes. "You love this dress. Admit it."

Ryerson summoned his most intimidating stare. Strong men had been known to break and bleed when Ryerson used that particular stare. "That dress is going in the trash tonight."

"Hah! That's what you think," Virginia said with relish.

"We'll see," Ryerson muttered, aware that he was not doing a very effective job of intimidation. It was tough to intimidate a goddess.

The music came to a halt, and Ryerson eased Virginia through the crowd to their table. He was about to continue the lecture on the dress when the man in the blue blazer approached them.

"Mind if I borrow the lady for the next dance?" Mustache asked with easy confidence. The question was officially addressed to Ryerson, but the stranger was looking at Virginia, who smiled back with sparkling innocence.

"Yes, I mind," Ryerson said roughly and added the first explanation that popped into his head. "The lady and I are on our honeymoon. I'm not in the mood to share."

The man's brows rose mockingly, and he made a point of glancing at Virginia's ringless hand. "Sorry about the intrusion. My name is Ferris. Dan Ferris. I didn't notice a ring so I assumed—"

"You assumed wrong," Ryerson cut in.

"Don't mind Ryerson, Mr. Ferris," Virginia said kindly. "He's in a bad mood because he doesn't like my dress."

The stranger nodded gallantly. A lot of white teeth gleamed beneath the mustache. "Personally I think the dress is very charming."

"Thank you."

"If you'll excuse us," Ryerson said bluntly, "we'd like to be alone."

"Sure. I understand. Well, congratulations on the marriage," Ferris said regretfully. "I guess that leaves me out of the picture."

"Oh, there is no marriage," Virginia said so sweetly that Ryerson was tempted to strangle her.

Ferris looked confused. "I thought there was something said about a honeymoon."

Ryerson caught one of Virginia's hands and crushed it warningly just as she opened her mouth to reply. He gave Ferris a baleful glance. "We're taking a few liberties with tradition. Whoever said a honeymoon had to come after the marriage? Good night, Ferris."

Ferris held up his hands, palms out in mocking surrender. "I get the point. I'm gone." He looked at Virginia again. "It really is a nice dress, though."

"I'm glad somebody likes it," Virginia said irrepressibly as Ferris disappeared in the crowd.

"Ninety-nine percent of the men in this room would be glad to tell you how much they like it if they got a chance." Ryerson got to his feet and pulled Virginia up out of her chair. Clamping a hand around her wrist, he started toward the door. "Come on, let's get out of here."

"Where are we going?"

"For a walk on the beach."

"At midnight?"

"I feel the need for some exercise," Ryerson told her grimly. "I would prefer to get it by making Ferris eat his own mustache, but I'll settle for a walk."

"Very civilized of you."

They walked in silence through the moonlight until they reached the endless stretch of white sand that ringed the island. Without a word they stopped and took off their shoes.

"Are you really angry about this dress?" Virginia asked finally.

Ryerson tightened his hand around hers. "Does it bother you that I'm acting like an overprotective, jealous male?" he countered. "Maybe I didn't handle that scene with Ferris properly. It's not my fault. I'm not used to feeling so possessive."

Virginia flashed him a molten glance. "I wore the dress to seduce you, you know. Maybe I overdid things. I'm not accustomed to dressing up to deliberately seduce men."

Ryerson felt the aggressive tension drain out of him as he stopped and gathered Virginia close. "So maybe we're both having to deal with some new emotions and reactions these days."

"Why did you tell Dan Ferris we were on a honeymoon?"

"I don't know," Ryerson admitted, aware of the lingering harshness in his voice. He could not really explain that stupid slip of the tongue. "I wanted to get rid of him as quickly as possible, and that was the first excuse that came to mind."

"Oh." She went still against him.

Ryerson tangled his hands in her hair. "The thought scares you, doesn't it?"

"Honeymoons and weddings and marriages are generally scary thoughts for me." She lifted her face and smiled tremulously up at him. "But I am very much enjoying having an affair."

"So am I," he muttered. He kissed her, tasting the moonlight he saw on her lips.

Her hands stole around his neck, and Ryerson felt her fingertips in his hair. Deliberately he crushed her closer so that he could feel her luscious, firm breasts against his chest. His hands slid down to the curve of her buttocks, and his mouth strayed to her throat. She felt so good. He was already hot and ready for her. He wanted her now.

Ryerson lifted his mouth from Virginia's and glanced down the length of the beach to where the lights of the resort gleamed in the distance. There was no one in sight.

"Ryerson? What are you doing?" Virginia gasped as she felt his fingers on the zipper of her dress.

"It's a great night for a swim."

She laughed up at him in astonishment. "We can't possibly. Not like this. We should go back to the hotel and get our suits."

"We're alone on this planet, remember?"

She sighed in pleasure and put her arms around his neck again as the gauzy dress fell to her bare feet. Moonlight gleamed on her breasts. "How could I forget?"

Ryerson shed his own clothing with casual disregard for sand and wrinkles. When he was naked, he picked up his quasi bride and carried her into the warm, silvered sea.

He didn't care how nervous the idea of marriage made Virginia. He did feel as though he were on a honeymoon, and he intended to enjoy it.

FIVE

The water was liquid silk. The only other thing Virginia had ever experienced that was as deliciously seductive was Ryerson's lovemaking. Swimming nude in the sea had the same effect on her senses. She shed old inhibitions as easily as she had shed her clothing.

She swam and frolicked around Ryerson, playing sea goddess in the silver moonlight. She had never felt so wild and free. It was as if she were another species of female altogether. And Ryerson was made for her, a helpless male on whom she could test her wiles.

Slipping and sliding through the waves, she circled her victim, taunting him with soft laughter and teasing touches. Ryerson responded with a primitive passion that thrilled her to the core of her being.

He reacted to the sweet torment with a deceptive clumsiness, tempting her closer until she recklessly came within reach. When at last she finally grew too bold and too careless, he seized her.

"Got you, sea lady. Now what are you going to do?" He held her by her waist, lifting her up out of the water so that she had to grip his shoulders to maintain her balance. His eyes gleamed with his victory.

Virginia smiled down at him with mischievous sensuality. "That's a good question," she murmured. "What would you like me to do?" Deliberately she drew slow circles on his damp shoulders. "You've won the battle. I'm yours to command." The water heaved gently around them, foaming lightly when it broke against her thighs. Her smile was very ancient and very pagan, and it disclosed everything she was feeling.

Ryerson saw the smile and sucked in his breath. The pale gleam of tropical moonlight revealed the stark desire on his face. "Mine to command?"

"Yours," she agreed softly. Virginia touched the side of his face. "What would you like me to do, sea lord? I want only to please you."

"I've never had a sea nymph at my disposal," Ryerson mused. "I'll have to experiment a little to find out what works best."

"By all means, feel free to experiment." Virginia felt her own excitement skyrocketing. "If I might make a few suggestions?"

"Anything," he breathed, his voice thickening rapidly. "Try anything you want. I'll let you know what's working."

"How about this?" She drew her fingertips down to his flat nipples and found them already puckered. When she gently scored him with her nails, Ryerson shuddered.

"That definitely works," Ryerson assured her. He lowered her slightly in the water until she was standing on the sandy bottom.

Virginia's smile became more mysterious as she experimented further. She trailed her fingertips through the hair on his chest and then slowly reached around his waist until she could sink her fingers into his hard, muscled buttocks. Deliberately she brushed against him, teasing Ryerson with her taut nipples.

"How about this?"

"I appreciate the suggestions," Ryerson said in a husky voice. "But I think I'm getting some ideas of my own."

"Tell me," she whispered. "I'll do anything you want."

He looked down at her with a searching gaze. "You mean that, don't you?"

"I mean every word. I want to please you tonight, Ryerson. I surrender completely to you, sea lord. I want only to make you happy."

"Touch me," he said hoarsely. "That will make me very happy."

"Where? Here?"

"Lower." He grinned with devilish challenge and told her graphically exactly what portion of his anatomy he wanted her to caress.

If his thought was to tease her or embarrass her, he had another think coming, Virginia decided bravely. Boldly she took him in her hands, playing with him under the surface of the foaming sea. Ryerson's wicked grin quickly disappeared.

"Ah, that's it. That's exactly where I want to feel your hands. You have such beautiful hands, sweetheart. I think I could really get into this conquering-hero bit." He drew in his breath as she squeezed gently. "*Yes*, honey. A little tighter. Perfect. Harder now. Faster."

Virginia gave him exactly what he wanted, delighting in her newly discovered power to do so. She kissed his salt-sprayed chest as she coaxed his body into a hard, heavy state of sexual expectation.

Ryerson tangled his fingers in her hair and slitted his eyes against the rush of excitement that was gripping his body. He pushed his hips against her, seeking more of her hand.

His powerful reaction fed her sense of feminine daring. Ryerson responded to her. Totally. It was a wonderful high for her. Virginia took a deep breath and sank gently beneath the waves.

She felt Ryerson's fingers tighten violently in her floating hair as she guided him into her mouth. His whole body was taut now. She knew he was about to explode.

"*Ginny.*" Abruptly he yanked her above the surface. His silver eyes were glittering. "You're a sea witch, all right. You've put me under a spell, and now you're going to put me out of my misery."

"Misery?" She laughed softly. "Is that what you call it? And here I was just trying to please."

He grinned with rough sensuality. "I'm not sure who's the conqueror and who's the sex slave around here right at the moment. But I do know one thing."

"What's that?"

"You're going to finish what you started."

"Of course, my lord. I wouldn't think of leaving you in this condition."

He cradled her face and kissed her heavily. "Wrap your legs around me," he ordered thickly.

Bemused, but willing, Virginia did as instructed. The water buoyed her and Ryerson's hands under her buttocks steadied her. She felt him slide two fingers into her, and then he hesitated no longer. She gasped as he entered her completely. Then she clung to him, burying her face against his throat. The sea surged around them, establishing the rhythm for them. It was a timeless cadence, one their bodies adjusted to automatically.

When the inevitable release tore through them, Virginia cried out. She was distantly aware of Ryerson's harsh, guttural shout echoing hers, and then there were only the sea and silence.

"I think," Ryerson finally said, "that we had better move toward shore."

"Why? I'm perfectly happy where I am." Without opening her eyes, Virginia nestled closer.

"There's a small but growing problem with staying where you are," he retorted with a chuckle as he carefully disengaged her.

"Really?" She was mildly interested. "A growing problem, did you say?" She tightened her legs around his thighs.

"Not that kind of problem," Ryerson explained wryly. "Another kind. The tide's coming in. In case you hadn't noticed, the water is getting deeper by the minute."

Virginia's eyes flicked open as she slid to her feet. The foaming water hit her now around the shoulders instead of the waist. "Good heavens! We could have come to a rather embarrassing end out here. Just think what people would have said at the funeral."

"It would have been a new twist on the old 'lost at sea' verdict. Come on; let's get moving, woman." Ryerson tugged her out of the surf.

The incoming tide was already lapping at their crumpled clothing. Virginia laughed as she struggled into her wet dress. "If you think this dress was a bit daring when it was dry, just wait until you see the effect now that it's soaking wet."

Ryerson scowled at the clinging material that revealed far more than it had earlier. Even in the shadows, he could see the clear outline of her nipples. When she turned around, he could easily make out the dark cleavage of her lush bottom. "I'm sure as hell not taking you back to the room via the main lobby. We'll go through the gardens." He fastened his pants and reached for his shirt.

Hand in hand they ran back along the beach, slipping into the hotel's gardens like two illicit lovers returning from a clandestine meeting.

"I think we were born for this kind of thing," Virginia said enthusiastically as Ryerson eased her soundlessly through a mass of huge ferns. "Look how good we are at sneaking around through the underbrush."

"I'm glad you're getting off on it," Ryerson said with mild irritation. "Personally I'm not into creeping around. If you hadn't worn that ridiculous excuse for a dress tonight, we wouldn't be in this position.... Shush—" He broke off suddenly.

"What in the world?" Virginia almost stumbled into him. He caught her, steadying her silently.

"We're not the only ones sneaking around through the bushes tonight. There're a couple of people up ahead." Ryerson's voice was a low whisper, containing none of the disgruntled humor it had held a few seconds earlier. "I think they're coming this way. Let's give them a chance to move on before we head for our room."

Obediently Virginia went still beside him, aware of the wet gauzy cotton turning cold against her skin. The clumps of ferns and flowering bushes hid them from the view of the two men who were striding briskly through the foliage. More people creeping around in the gardens. She wondered what their excuse was for not sticking to the stone paths.

Virginia caught only a brief glimpse of two masculine heads bent in intense conversation, but she recognized the voices immediately. Harry Brigman and Dan Ferris. Ferris's voice cut through the balmy night.

"Dammit, Brigman, we've fooled around here long enough. You've had your fun. I'm getting nervous. We've done all right. It's time to get the hell off this island."

"There's no rush. I've told you that a hundred times. We have to cool our heels somewhere. It might as well be here on Toralina. Besides, this place is ripe for the picking. Lots of rich tourists just begging for a friendly game of poker."

"There are other islands with casinos. Hell, you don't even need a casino. You can set up a game anywhere, as long as you're discreet."

"I like it here," Brigman said stubbornly. "I've been on a winning streak since I arrived."

"You didn't win the other night when you played Ryerson. Exactly how much did you lose, Brigman?"

"Not enough to concern you," Brigman retorted sullenly. "It was just a temporary setback. The man got lucky. It happens occasionally. But he's not a real pro. I'll talk him into another game and get my money back before he leaves. Now, if you'll excuse me, I've got some people waiting for me in the casino. It's about time you got on with your end of things, isn't it?"

Whatever Ferris said in response was muffled as both men moved off through the bushes.

"Okay," Ryerson said softly after a few seconds. "There's the path up ahead. Let's go. But keep it quiet."

"This is so exciting," Virginia said happily. "I wonder if we—oh, no!" She yelped helplessly and tried to keep her balance as the wet skirts of her dress snagged on a jagged palm frond. "Darn it, my new dress! It's ruined."

Ryerson muttered a resigned oath and turned to untangle the torn dress. As he swung around to assist, he glanced automatically toward where the two men had disappeared. "Damn. So much for sneaking around in the gardens."

"Why? What's wrong?" Virginia followed his gaze and caught a glimpse of Dan Ferris, who must have stepped out onto the path a few seconds ahead of them. Ferris paused for an instant and glanced back over his shoulder when he overheard her startled cry. He looked directly at her. "Oh, dear. Well, can't be helped. And no real harm done. It's not as if I'm naked." She smiled and waved cheerfully at Ferris, who nodded brusquely and disappeared around a bend in the path. Brigman had already vanished.

"No, it's not as if you're naked." Ryerson freed the snagged material. "But it's the next best thing. Good thing Ferris was a long way down that path or he'd have gotten an eyeful. The way that wet material is clinging to you, a man can see just about everything."

Virginia arched her brows as she realized where Ryerson's own eyes were focused. "Only a man with exceptionally good night vision could see *everything*."

"I must have exceptionally good night vision."

"Either that or an overactive imagination. You know, I didn't realize those two even knew each other," Virginia remarked as Ryerson urged her out of the bushes.

"Neither did I." Ryerson sounded thoughtful. "I wonder why they were running around out here in the gardens?" Then his voice changed. "Come on, let's get into a hot shower. You're getting cold."

"How did you know?"

Ryerson chuckled and deliberately traced a blunt fingertip over the rigid outline of one of her nipples. "My terrific night vision."

* * *

Ryerson successfully ignored Brigman's offer of a card game right up until the last night of the vacation. He was not even vaguely tempted, as he had been the first time around. Having won the bracelet, Ryerson was more than content. Brigman was right. He was no cardplayer. He'd just gotten very lucky one night. Now his luck lay in other directions.

On the last night of their stay, Virginia had a few qualms. She touched the bracelet protectively as they moved out onto the dance floor. Then she glanced toward where Brigman was playing cards in the casino.

"Do you think the bracelet really is a family heirloom?" she asked Ryerson.

"It may be somebody's family heirloom, but I'd bet Middlebrook Power Systems that it doesn't belong in Brigman's family."

Ryerson spoke with such conviction that Virginia relaxed. "You're sure?"

"Why would he be traipsing around the Caribbean with a valuable heirloom? The man's a professional card shark, Ginny. He won that bracelet from someone else. And now it's ours. Fortunes of war."

She breathed a sigh of relief and glanced at the beautiful stones. "And now it's ours," she repeated.

Ryerson followed her gaze and smiled possessively. "Think of it as a souvenir of the start of our affair."

Virginia gazed down at the gems shimmering on her wrist. When she lifted her eyes again, her smile had become a little less certain. "I wonder if things will be the same when we go home tomorrow."

The possessive pleasure that had been in Ryerson's eyes as he looked at the bracelet faded away slightly. "What the hell do you mean by that?"

She shifted uneasily in his arms. "I don't know. Somehow everything seems so different here on Toralina. You said yourself it's as if we're two different people in a different world. I guess I'm wondering whether it will last after we return to Seattle."

Ryerson wrapped his hands around her nape and used his thumbs to lift her face so that she had to meet his eyes. His silvery gaze was intent and full of a fierce energy. "We're the same two people we were before we left Seattle. The only thing that changed for us here on Toralina is that we started sleeping together. I'll tell you right now that's not going to change back when we reach Seattle."

Ryerson awoke an hour before dawn. It wasn't the faint glow in the sky that brought him out of a sensual dream of making love to Virginia. It was the soft sound of footsteps on the tile in the outer room. Someone had broken into the suite. Utter quiet followed the small noises.

Ryerson sat up slowly and silently. But Virginia must have sensed his movement because she stirred and started to open her eyes. He covered her lips with his palm. Her lashes lifted in alarm.

There was just enough light in the room for him to shake his head in silent warning. She didn't move, just stared at him intently. He knew she had gotten the message.

The faint sound came again from the other room. This time Virginia heard it, too. She stiffened but said nothing as he took his hand away from her mouth.

Indicating with his hand that she was to remain unmoving, Ryerson eased slowly off the bed and got to his feet. Naked, he padded toward where the door to the other room stood slightly ajar. When he glanced through the crack, he caught the flickering beam of a tiny, narrow flashlight. A figure moved briefly into view. Ryerson saw nothing in the man's free hand. As far as he could tell, whoever the prowler was, he was unarmed.

Ryerson slid one arm out to the side and touched the dresser. His hand closed around the handle of Virginia's travel-size blow dryer. It wasn't much, but it was all that was available. The sturdy plastic nozzle should be capable of inflicting some damage. He started to ease open the door and simultaneously heard a drawer close in the outer room.

Ryerson hadn't seen a gun, but as he leaped through the door he belatedly wondered what the hell he was going to do if the prowler pulled a knife. Something about launching a defensive assault without even a pair of undershorts on had a disturbing effect on a man's concentration.

The thought of whoever was in the other room getting past him to attack Virginia, however, was a powerful motivator.

The figure at the writing desk spun around with a hoarse, hissing sound of dismay as Ryerson came through the door. The prowler was wearing a stocking mask. He threw up his hands in an instinctive attempt to ward off his attacker and then he plunged for the door.

Ryerson was only a split second behind him, but that instant was enough to enable the prowler to clear the door and race out into the dark safety of the gardens.

Ryerson was halfway through the door when a movement in the bedroom doorway brought him to a brief, slamming halt. Virginia stood there, her eyes huge and anxious. He saw she was clutching a high-heeled shoe in one hand as a weapon. She was as nude as he was except for the faint glitter of the bracelet on her wrist. She had insisted on wearing the thing to bed, as usual.

"Call the front desk," Ryerson ordered tersely. "Have them get the cops." He didn't wait for a response.

A few minutes later, Ryerson had occasion to reconsider the wisdom of dashing out into the gardens without a stitch on. He lost his quarry almost at once. The man disappeared quickly in the thick foliage that enveloped the hotel. But the commotion caught the attention of a young man in a white hotel uniform who was obviously just returning from a late-night room service delivery.

"Mind loaning me a napkin?" Ryerson asked grimly as the young man stared in openmouthed amazement.

"Of course, sir." The young man recovered his aplomb immediately. He had obviously been in the resort business long enough to know that one could expect almost anything from the guests. He deftly plucked a large pink napkin from the tray and offered it to Ryerson with a proper flourish.

"Thank you. Suite 316. Have the front desk put a couple of bucks extra on my bill for your tip." Ryerson turned and strode back toward the room with the napkin held discreetly in front of him and the blow dryer cocked at a rakish angle. The important thing, he reminded himself, was to appear casual and nonchalant.

The Toralina police were sincerely regretful of the incident but were unable to do much about it. These things happened occasionally, they explained with great sadness, and just lately they'd been troubled with a rash of hotel prowlers. It was probably an out-of-work island fisherman or farm laborer who had had a little too much rum or tequila before getting up the nerve to go through the hotel rooms where the rich people from the States stayed. The police would certainly keep an eye out, but since there was little or no description there really wasn't much to go on, et cetera, et cetera.

"Something tells me the case was closed the minute we boarded the plane," Ryerson said through his teeth as he fastened his seat belt a few hours later.

"Stop worrying about it," Virginia soothed. "Nothing was taken, thanks to you." She gave him an ingenuous smile. "My hero. If I live to be a hundred, I'll never forget the sight of you racing off naked after the bad guy and returning with a pink napkin."

But Ryerson was not in the mood for jokes yet. He stared out the window, watching the lush island landscape fall away as the jet lifted off the runway. "I wonder what he was after."

"Wallets, jewelry or anything else a hotel guest might have stashed in his room," Virginia said. "Let's be honest, Ryerson. The people who live on this island live in a different world from those of us who vacation here. There's a lot of poverty in the Caribbean."

"Jewelry," Ryerson repeated softly. "I wonder if whoever it was knew about the bracelet."

"How could he? We didn't open the box in front of anyone. The only one who knew you'd won the bracelet from Brigman was Brigman himself."

"That's right," Ryerson said meaningfully.

"You don't think Brigman tried to get his bracelet back last night, do you?"

"It's a possibility. He wasn't pleased about losing it to me in that card game, and he turned downright sullen when I kept refusing his offer of a rematch."

"It was Brigman who insisted on that first game of cards, and he didn't have to bet the bracelet. You won it from him fair and square, and it's ours now," Virginia declared, feeling very possessive. She clutched her purse more tightly. She had the emerald bracelet safely tucked into an inside pocket of her bag.

Ryerson glanced at her, and then his mouth curved enigmatically as he reached out and took Virginia's hand. "You're right," he agreed quietly. "It's ours now."

"You're sure we won't have trouble bringing it in through customs?"

"No. I checked. Anything over a hundred years old gets into the States duty free. And the jeweler's appraisal report we found in the box verifies that the bracelet is too old to concern customs."

"It's really ours," Virginia said again. "I can hardly believe it." But the truth was, it was even harder to believe in what she had found with Ryerson. That was the real treasure she was bringing back from Toralina.

SIX

Not until she was back into the routine of her daily life did Virginia allow herself to admit just how nervous she had been about returning home. She had felt like a different person on Toralina, and a part of her had wondered uneasily if she would revert to the woman she had been before the trip once she was back in her normal surroundings.

But as she dressed for a dinner date with Ryerson a week after the trip back to Seattle, Virginia looked at herself in the mirror and smiled with secret delight. She had changed, and the change appeared to be permanent, even if it wasn't clearly definable. It was there in her eyes, and she knew Ryerson could see it, just as she could. The change was visible in other ways, too.

The dress she was wearing tonight was not as daring as the infamous one Ryerson had disapproved of on Toralina, but it was decidedly more adventuresome in style than the sort Virginia had been accustomed to buying before she went to the Caribbean. It was true the bra and panties underneath were still made of functional, plain white cotton, but things were changing.

The woman who looked back at her from the mirror was far more confident now in her sexuality. She was bolder, more free spirited. The woman who had swum naked in the sea off Toralina Island was quite capable of contemplating sitting nude in a hot tub with A. C. Ryerson, for example.

Unfortunately neither she nor Ryerson had a hot tub.

But that was a mere detail, Virginia thought as she started to fasten the bracelet in place on her wrist. The point was, she could actually consider the idea.

The light flashed on a small mark inside the clasp of the bracelet. Virginia paused and gazed at it closely. It was a tiny crest, she realized. Someday it might be interesting to see if a jeweler could identify it.

An hour later when she was seated across from Ryerson at a cozy restaurant in the old section of Seattle known as Pioneer Square, she decided to bring up the subject that had been on her mind earlier.

"Have you ever thought about putting in a hot tub?" she asked breezily, chewing on a bread stick that had just been brought to the table.

Ryerson glanced up from buttering his own bread stick. There was a flicker of surprise and then a suspicious glitter in his eyes. "A hot tub? Now that you mention it, no. I've never considered the idea. Until now, that is." He paused thoughtfully, his gaze drifting to the bracelet on her wrist. "It could be done. There's a spot that would be perfect for it at my island place. I want to take you out there soon, by the way. What made you start thinking of hot tubs?"

Virginia shrugged innocently. "I was just remembering that night we went swimming in the sea and that thought just sort of naturally turned to hot tubs."

"A logical chain of thought," Ryerson said approvingly. He chomped down on the bread stick, his strong white teeth snapping it neatly. "You know, I can see us sitting in that hot tub right now."

Virginia smiled demurely. "Really? What does the image do for you?"

"Makes me hot as hell. You really want to finish dinner, or can we go straight back to my condo now?"

Virginia nearly choked on her laughter. "Ryerson, we haven't even started dinner and I'm hungry."

He sighed with mocking regret. "Okay, okay, I guess I can wait. I wonder how long it takes to install a hot tub. I could handle the pump motor installation myself. All I would need is the tub. If I called someone in the morning and could get it delivered to the island quickly enough . . ."

"Forget about trying to install a hot tub this weekend," Virginia said on a laugh. "We have to go to the Andersons' party on Sunday, remember? You specifically asked me to go with you to introduce you to people." The Andersons were old business friends of the Middlebrook family, and one of the reasons they were giving the party this weekend, Virginia suspected, was to welcome the new owner of Middlebrook Power Systems.

"You're right. Business before pleasure. I'll worry about the hot tub later. I've got other things on my mind tonight, anyway." The sexy humor faded from his gaze to be replaced by something much more serious. "You are planning to stay the night with me, aren't you?"

"I brought some things in an overnight bag," she admitted softly.

Ryerson relaxed. "I hoped that gym bag you had in the car wasn't really full of old sweats and dirty sneakers. Ginny, I think it's time we talked about moving in together."

Wine splashed precariously in the glass Virginia had just picked up. She tensed. "Move in together? You and me?"

"I wasn't talking about getting a cat," he muttered. "Of course I meant you and me. Think about it, Ginny. It's the next logical step in our relationship. This business of commuting on the ferry is going to get old really quickly. It's already made things damned difficult this week. Next week probably won't be any better. I've got some late meetings and an early-morning appointment with a potential client."

Virginia felt her insides twist. Her first shattering thought was that Ryerson was getting bored with her almost as quickly as her husband had. The confidence she had gained on Toralina began to dissipate. Virginia made a grab to hang on to it. She fought to keep calm and not jump to conclusions. This was Ryerson, not Jack.

"You're getting impatient with the commuting problem already?" she asked unsteadily. "But we've hardly even begun our relationship. I mean, we've just been back from Toralina for a few days. I thought we were getting along well together. I thought you were happy. I thought things were going nicely. I didn't realize you were getting bored."

"Sweet hell, lady, you're not listening to me." Ryerson's eyes narrowed abruptly as he realized what she was thinking. All the joy had evaporated from her face. She was watching him now with a deep wariness that tore him apart. It also angered him. "I'm asking you to move in with me. I'm not suggesting we call a halt to our affair. Just the opposite. What's the matter with you? Can't you understand plain English?"

She put her hands in her lap. Ryerson couldn't see what she was doing, but he was willing to bet she was crushing her napkin into a crumpled ball. Her face was strained.

"You said the commute to my place was going to get old. I assumed that meant you were already getting bored with the idea," Virginia said stiffly.

"And from that you deduced that I was getting bored with you." Ryerson shook his head in disgust. "Your logic is screwy, but I'm willing to overlook that for the moment. The topic I'm trying to cover here is very simple and straightforward. Ginny, I'm asking you to consider moving in with me. I am not getting bored with the commute. I am finding it a pain in the ass. There's a difference."

"What's the difference?"

Ryerson wondered if there was any law against a man shaking some sense into his woman in a public restaurant. He assumed there was. "The difference is this: when I am bored with a situation, I get out of that situation as fast as possible. When I am finding something to be a pain in the rear, I look for a way to fix the problem. The way to fix this particular problem is for us to live together."

Virginia was eyeing him cautiously now. "You want us to try living together?"

"Congratulations. You are now beginning to grasp the concept," he retorted as the salad arrived. He watched her chew on her thoughts as the waiter arranged the plates.

"Living together would be a lot like marriage," she said finally, making no move to pick up her fork as the waiter left.

Ryerson recognized the direction of her thoughts. He had moved too quickly. If she knew just how quickly he wanted to move, she would be literally terrified. He looked for a way to reassure her.

"Virginia," he stated in his best lecturing tone, the one he used to sell doubtful clients on the merits of diesel engines, "living together is not like marriage. Not a bit. Granted, there are a few of the advantages of marriages, but . . ."

"And all the disadvantages," she concluded quickly.

He scowled at her. "Not necessarily."

"Have you tried it with anyone else?" she demanded.

"Well, no, but it's easy to see how it could work very well for two people like us."

"I don't see how it would be any different than marriage," she insisted.

Ryerson was beginning to lose his patience, which was rare for him. "You're being willfully stubborn about this. I can see you're anxious. Trust me. Living together is fundamentally different from being married to each other."

"I don't see how." She waved a hand in a small, desperate little movement and leaned forward intently. "Think about it. Living together would involve everything from sharing expenses to relatives. It would mean figuring out who would do the laundry this week and who would clean the bathroom. It would mean breakfast every morning together. It would mean sharing *closet* space, for heaven's sake. Do you realize what you're talking about here? I'd take over half of your dresser drawers. I'd leave dirty coffee cups in your sink. I'd fill up your bathroom with my shampoo and cosmetics and deodorant. Living together would not be like sharing a hotel room on Toralina. It would be much more complicated."

Ryerson almost laughed aloud at the frantic look on her face. The only thing that stopped him was the knowledge that she was so serious. "The idea really traumatizes you, doesn't it?"

She sat back in her chair, her eyes watchful. "I find it very unsettling. It goes against everything we've decided we want out of this relationship."

"It might go against everything you think you want out of this relationship, but it doesn't bother me in the least. I don't have your bias against marriage, remember?"

"That's right. You think it would be a very comfortable arrangement with the right person, don't you?" she shot back. "And you probably feel the same way about living together. You think it would be comfortable. But that's probably not the way it would be. All the problems would be exposed. All the little things that can be overlooked while we're having an affair would become major nuisances if we lived together. Some of those little things might prove to be more important than you realize. You might not be able to tolerate them."

He was getting nowhere fast. Ryerson backed off temporarily. "Ginny, all I'm doing is asking you to think about it. I guarantee it would not be the same as getting married. There would be no formal commitment, for one thing. You would not be trapped in any way. We'll go into it slowly. I'll let you get your feet wet gradually, if you like."

"How?" she asked suspiciously.

"You don't have to move in all at once," he said persuasively. "We'll take it in stages. Try spending some portion of the next few weeks here in town with me and we'll see how it goes."

"But everything's working so well the way it is," she wailed. "We're happy this way."

"You think living together will really spoil what we have?" A quiet anger began to simmer inside him. He had been so certain he could overcome her fears.

"I don't know," she whispered.

He realized she was genuinely frightened of the whole notion. Far more so than he had imagined she would be. Hell, he hadn't even broached marriage yet. Until now he had assumed her resistance to the idea of marriage was a minor thing that would be easily handled with a little trust, passion and time.

His long-range plan had been to introduce her to the notion of marriage slowly through a living-together arrangement that would allay her old fears. He had assumed the passion between them would give him all the leverage he needed. Time would do the rest. Now he wasn't so sure. The woman was just plain scared.

"Your husband did a real number on you," Ryerson said, aware of the impotent fury inside him. "If he weren't already dead and gone, I'd be tempted to look him up and give him a hand with his departure."

Virginia looked taken aback by his vehemence. "Ryerson, I thought you understood how I felt about marriage."

Ryerson lost his temper. "For the last time," he said forcefully, "I am not talking about marriage. *I am talking about living together.*" A sudden silence in the atmosphere around them made him realize that his words had been clearly overheard by neighboring diners. Several surreptitious glances were cast in his direction, some amused, some curious and some distinctly disapproving. "We will finish this conversation later when we're alone," Ryerson ground out between his teeth.

Virginia hesitated, looking as if she wanted to say more, but she must have seen the grim determination in his eyes because she wisely held her peace.

The meal was finished in near silence. Ryerson alternately cursed himself for having ruined the evening and then reminded himself that he had to start somewhere. He had known when he came back from Toralina that he would never be content unless he had Virginia living under his roof. That wasn't the end of it, either. The raw truth was that he would not be content until he had her committed to marriage.

The emerald bracelet glittered in the lamplight as she lifted her wineglass. Ryerson glanced at the old piece of jewelry. It looked good on her, he thought. It called attention to her graceful hands and delicate wrists.

Dammit, he had to pin Virginia down. He had to find a way to talk her into his home as well as into his bed. She should realize by now that he was different from her dead husband. She was going to have to learn to trust him.

The green flames flared in the depths of the gems, beckoning and promising and enticing. He stared at the bracelet.

"Is something wrong?" Virginia asked uneasily, seeing the direction of his gaze.

Ryerson shook his head, frowning as he realized how intently he had been studying the bracelet. "No, nothing's wrong. Are you ready to leave?"

She nodded. "I'm ready."

"Then let's get out of here." He pulled out his wallet and located a charge card. "It's time we went home." He used the word *home* deliberately, testing her to see if she would bristle in reaction.

But Virginia said nothing. She finished her wine in silence while Ryerson scrawled his name on the charge slip.

Virginia tried hard to forget what had been said in the restaurant. On the way back to Ryerson's condominium, she made a concerted effort to introduce bright, cheerful, nonthreatening topics of conversation.

Ryerson ignored her part of the time and gave her monosyllabic responses when he did deign to participate in the conversation. He maintained a dark, brooding silence as they drove through the old brick structures that dominated Pioneer Square. It was Friday night, and the area was filling with the crowd who had come to this part of town to enjoy the small theaters, restaurants and the numerous taverns with their popular jazz and rock bands.

Ryerson held his peace as he drove north on First Avenue toward his high-rise condominium building. He still didn't say a word as he parked the Mercedes in the garage and escorted Virginia into the elevator.

When they reached his floor, he shoved the key into the lock, opened the door and stood aside to allow Virginia into the darkened apartment. She went in quickly, sneaking an uneasy glance at his hard face.

"Ryerson," she said softly as he closed and locked the door behind him, "I think we had better talk. We need to settle this."

He eyed her as he shrugged out of his jacket. "We've done enough talking for now. It's obvious we're not communicating in some areas. Might as well stick to the one area in which we do communicate." He loosened his tie.

Virginia took a step back, unsure of the expression in his eyes. She could usually read this man like a book. It was one of the things she liked about the relationship. She felt she understood Ryerson. But tonight she was not so certain.

"I disagree," she said with a calm she was far from feeling. He had the tie undone and was unbuttoning his shirt. "This business of living together is clearly going to be an issue. I hadn't realized you were even thinking in those terms. It changes everything. We must talk it out."

He came toward her deliberately, not bothering to turn on any lights. His shirt was hanging open. In the shadowy room the roughly hewn features of his face were cast into forbidding lines. His eyes were trapped pools of moonlight. He reached for her, his hands closing over her shoulders. Without a word he pulled her to him and captured her mouth. The kiss was heavy, thorough and deep.

All thought of protest and rational discussion faded from Virginia's mind. "Maybe you're right," she whispered dazedly against his lips when he finally raised his head. "Maybe this is the best way for us to communicate."

His body was hard and taut against hers. She felt his fingers tighten on her soft shoulders. "Don't get the idea that you can distract me with sex every time we're on the verge of arguing about our future," he warned harshly.

She shook her head quickly. "I didn't mean that. Besides, it was you who cut off the conversation a minute ago."

"True. I just thought I ought to warn you that we will be returning to it, sooner or later."

"But not right now?" she asked hopefully.

"Right now," he told her, "I've developed other priorities." He picked her up in his arms and carried her down the hall to his bedroom.

Hours later Virginia awoke in the darkness, aware of a burning thirst and a bad headache. Her first thought was that she must have had too much to drink at dinner. She lay quietly for a moment, trying to figure out why the room did not look familiar.

Her stomach was churning. She frowned, remembering that she had had only two glasses of wine earlier. Whatever was causing the headache and the nausea couldn't be related to overindulgence.

She turned her head restlessly on the pillow, annoyed because the normal outline of her bedroom would not come into focus. Maybe she was dreaming.

She was so warm. It was far too hot in here tonight. Virginia shoved aside the sheet and blanket. She had to open a window.

It wasn't until she tried to sit up that she finally began to realize something was really wrong. She was dizzy. When she got to her feet she almost collapsed. She felt the carpet on the floor and knew it wasn't the rug in her own bedroom. Then she saw the heavy, dark shape on the bed.

She was in Ryerson's bedroom.

Relieved that she had finally figured out what was wrong with the room, Virginia took a grip on her whirling senses and aimed for the window. She wondered how Ryerson could sleep in such heat.

Her stomach threatened to betray her halfway to the window. Virginia wavered for a moment and then changed course for the bathroom. First things first. She was going to be violently sick.

Sick. She was ill. The room was not too hot; she was feverish. Horror shafted through her. She couldn't be sick. Not here. Jack had hated it when she was sick. Virginia staggered to the bathroom and closed the door behind her. She barely made it to the commode.

A few minutes later, the spasms were over. Shaking, Virginia clung to the sink, rinsing out her mouth while she tried to gather her senses and think.

She had to get out of Ryerson's apartment. She must not let him see her like this. If Ryerson saw her like this he would be disgusted and impatient with her, just as Jack had been.

This was one of the many reasons she could not take the risk of living with him, Virginia reminded herself as she forced herself to move to the bathroom door. A stupid thing like her getting sick would spoil everything.

She looked around frantically, knowing she had to get out of the condominium. She had to get back to the safety and comfort of her own home where she could be ill without the added burden of worrying about Ryerson's reaction to that illness.

The pain in her head was excruciating, but at least her stomach seemed temporarily under control. If only she didn't feel so hot and dizzy. It took every ounce of willpower Virginia possessed to stagger back into the bedroom and find her clothing. Ryerson did not move on the bed. The man was sleeping like a bear in winter.

Out in the living room, she concentrated hard on dressing. It was no easy task. Her fingers were shaking, and she kept having to steady herself to keep from losing her balance. It seemed to take forever to get the zipper of her dress pulled up.

When she was finished, Virginia stood panting for a moment, trying to catch her breath. Then she glanced around thinking vaguely that she should leave some sort of note. Ryerson would awake in the morning and wonder where she had gone.

With the aid of the pale light filtering in through the windows, she managed to locate a pad of paper and a pen near the telephone. She turned on the lamp and stared at the paper, trying to compose her thoughts. She could not think of anything to write for a long moment. After concentrating fiercely she finally put down, "Dear Ryerson. Had to go home. I'll call."

It wasn't much of a note, but it was all she could manage. Virginia switched off the lamp and started toward the door. When she stepped into the hallway she collided with a large, warm, immovable object. The object was naked and quite obviously male.

"Going somewhere?" Ryerson asked far too blandly.

Virginia nearly lost her balance. She clutched his arm to steady herself. He made no move to assist her. She released him at once and leaned against the wall.

"Have to go home," she whispered.

"You were going to leave without bothering to wake me? Very considerate."

She could hear the anger in him but she was too weak to react to it. "Left a note."

"I'm touched."

"Ryerson, please. I have to go home." She closed her eyes as she propped herself against the wall.

"Why do you have to go home at three in the morning?" Ryerson asked roughly. "Because you're panicked at the thought of spending even one night under my roof? You didn't feel obliged to go rushing off in the middle of the night while we were on Toralina. Or was that different because you were enjoying the free vacation I was providing?"

"Please." She tried to ease past him but he did not budge. "I have to go home."

"How do you plan to get there? The ferry stopped running an hour ago. There won't be another one until morning. How were you going to get to the docks, anyway? Steal my car?"

She hadn't thought clearly enough to figure out how to get to the ferry docks, Virginia realized. "I'll call a cab."

"Not much point, is there? I just told you, there's no ferry until six-thirty."

The words finally penetrated her brain. No car and no ferry. She was trapped. Virginia licked her dry lips, trying to think. "I'll call my sister."

"No, you damned well will not call your sister." Ryerson's fury was barely leashed now. "If you think you can spend the night in my bed and then sneak out before dawn, I've got news for you. I'm not going to let you get away with it. You owe me a lot more than that. What is it with you, Ginny? You want to be able to have your cake and eat it, too, don't you? Now that you've discovered the pleasures of sex, you want more, but you don't want to pay the price in terms of commitment."

"You don't understand." Dear Lord, she was going to collapse if he didn't get out of the way.

"That's what you think," Ryerson said bitterly. "I'm finally beginning to understand what's going on. You're too damned selfish or too scared or some combination of both to make a commitment of any kind to me, but you like what you find in my arms, don't you?"

"Ryerson, please, I must go."

He ignored that. "You like sex with me well enough to accept a trip to Toralina or a dinner at an expensive restaurant from me, but you won't accept any real bonds. You know what that makes you, Ginny?"

"Stop it," she breathed, a tiny flame of anger giving her a small shot of energy. "Stop calling me names. Just get out of my way. I'm leaving."

"The hell you are. You're going to stay right here in my home and in my bed until you learn you have to give as well as take if you want an affair with me."

Ryerson moved, reaching out to catch hold of Virginia's arm. She struggled briefly and the effort cost her what was left of her energy. The darkness whirled around her.

"*Ginny!*" Ryerson caught and held her as she collapsed. "You're burning up. What's wrong?"

"Tried to get out of here. I tried. You wouldn't let me go." Virginia turned her head fretfully. "I'm hot. Need a drink of water."

"A drink of water isn't going to put out the fire that's burning in you, honey. We need a little more help than that." He eased her down into a chair. "Wait right here while I get some clothes on."

"Why?" The chair was uncomfortable.

"Because I'm going to take you to an emergency room and the hospital staff would probably prefer I didn't walk in naked with you in my arms."

Hospital. "I don't want to go to the hospital. I'm all right."

"Sure you are. And I'm the lead dancer for the Pacific Northwest Ballet." Ryerson spoke from the bedroom where he was pulling on a pair of jeans and a shirt.

Virginia sat huddled in the chair, too feverish to even cry. Everything was going wrong. "All right," she whispered in defeat, "I'll call a cab to take me to the hospital."

"A cab will take too long at this hour." Ryerson strode back out into the hall, checking for his keys and wallet. "Can you walk or do you want me to carry you down to the garage?"

"I'll walk." She got unsteadily to her feet. There was no point arguing further. He was determined. Virginia surrendered to the inevitable. This might be the beginning of the end of the affair, but she could no longer fight it. "Oh, Ryerson, I feel so awful."

He steadied her with his arm about her shoulders as he half walked, half carried her to the elevator. "Stop worrying, honey. You're going to be fine. I'll get you to the emergency room and they'll give you something to break the fever. Then I'll bring you home and put you to bed."

"Home? You mean you'll take me back to my place?" she asked. Maybe there was hope, after all.

"I said home. I meant here. My home. You're not in any condition to be left on your own."

"But, Ryerson . . ."

"Hush, Ginny. I'm taking over now."

SEVEN

"Food poisoning." If Virginia hadn't been so drowsy, she knew she would have been even more indignant. Two hours after leaving for the emergency room, she was back in Ryerson's bed with the probable verdict. "I can't believe it. It was such a good restaurant!"

"They weren't absolutely certain it was food poisoning," Ryerson reminded her. "It might be the flu. You heard the doctor—it's hard to diagnose gastrointestinal disorders. They just treat the symptoms and let nature take its course."

"It's food poisoning," Virginia said firmly. "I'm starting to feel better already. If it was the flu, I'd feel worse. I'll tell you one thing: I'll never go back to that restaurant again."

"It might have been caused by whatever you had for lunch. One of the nurses said it can take several hours for the symptoms to show up." Ryerson moved efficiently around the room, plumping pillows and adjusting the blinds. "It can happen in the best of restaurants. If it is food poisoning."

"I'm voting for food poisoning."

Ryerson grinned. "You're not the only one who's voting for food poisoning. If it's the flu, I'll probably be joining you in bed soon, and as much as I'd enjoy the excuse I'd prefer not to be feeling nauseated when I'm making love to you."

She looked up at him, still a little uneasy about the situation. There was no doubt but that Ryerson had been wonderful. He had been calm and caring, and he had handled everything in the emergency room. He did not seem the least put off by having to play nurse.

"I'm sorry to be such a nuisance," she murmured, hugging the sheet to her chin. She was still suffering from occasional chills.

Ryerson gave her an exasperated look. "For the last time, stop worrying about it and stop apologizing for it. If you say one more word about being a nuisance, I'm liable to lose my temper. I'm going to make some tea. I'll be back in a few minutes."

Virginia nodded, still not trusting herself to speak. She closed her eyes and dozed until she sensed his presence beside the bed. "Thank you," she said, sitting up against the pillows to accept the teacup.

"You're welcome." Ryerson sat down on the bed, a mug in his big fist. "Are you feeling well enough to talk?"

"What do you want to talk about?"

"I think you know the answer to that. Now that the crisis is past, I'd like to know why you felt obliged to try to sneak out of here when you woke up so sick you could hardly stand."

Virginia focused on the dawn-lit sky outside the window. "I didn't know how my being ill would affect you," she finally admitted. "My husband couldn't stand sickness in others. He could be very cruel about it. Once when I had a bad cold, he told me I looked ten years older. He insisted I stay with my sister until I was well."

"So you just naturally figured I'd react the same way—is that it?"

Virginia flinched at the cool disgust in his tone. "A part of me didn't want to take any chances," she said honestly. "I didn't want you to see me like this. I didn't want to ruin things between us."

"You mean you didn't trust me to be able to tolerate your being sick. What kind of a man do you think I am, Ginny? We're involved with each other. In my book, that means we take care of each other."

She sighed. "An affair isn't marriage. An affair is based mostly on fantasy. Things seemed to be working for us on that level. I thought it best if reality didn't intrude."

"Tell me something, if I had been the one who had gotten sick tonight, would you have tried to ship me home before I became too big a problem?"

Her eyes flew to his. "Of course not," she said instantly. "How could you possibly think that?"

"Guess where I got the idea?" he replied laconically.

"But that's different," Virginia tried to explain.

"Is that right? Why? Because you're a woman, and women are just naturally nurturing? Bull. I'm demanding equal rights, you little female chauvinist. This attitude of yours is obviously another legacy left to you by your dead husband. Get rid of it. You're going to have to learn to trust me."

"But, Ryerson . . ."

Ryerson said something rude under his breath. "Ginny, you'd better face some obvious facts. There is no way for two people like us to have an affair and still stay free of all obligations and commitments. It doesn't work that way. We can't live in a total fantasy. Even if it's possible for some people, it's not possible for us. We're not the right types. We're too practical by nature. Things might have seemed unreal for a while down on Toralina, but that feeling won't last long now that we're home. Reality does intrude sooner or later, no matter how hard you try to guard against it. I, for one, have nothing against reality. The truth is, I'm better equipped to handle reality than I am a full-blown fantasy. And I think you are, too."

She hesitated and then leaned back against the pillow, closing her eyes. She thought of how sick she had been during the night and of how well he had handled everything. It was the way she would have handled things if the situation had been reversed. He was just like her in so many ways. "Yes," she said softly, "I'm beginning to see that."

There was silence for a long moment, and then Ryerson said calmly, "When you're feeling better, we'll talk about the details of moving you in with me."

In her mind Virginia heard the door of a velvet cage swing open invitingly. Maybe it would work, she thought for the first time. Ryerson was different. Maybe, just maybe, she could take the risk of living with Ryerson.

After all, if it didn't work out, they both would still technically be free. Perhaps she had been wrong earlier when she had argued against living together. Maybe living together wouldn't be quite the same thing as being married.

Or would it?

Virginia fell asleep with the question whirling in her mind.

For a long while, Ryerson sat watching Virginia with brooding, thoughtful eyes.

It still shook him to remember how he had felt in the early hours when he had awakened abruptly and realized she was trying to sneak out of the condo. He had been torn between rage and anguish. No doubt about it, Virginia was a living example of the once-bitten-twice-shy syndrome. She was going to drag her pretty heels every inch of the way.

Quietly he collected the tea mugs and started to leave the bedroom. He was halfway to the door when he saw Virginia's purse standing open on the nightstand. Green-and-white fire laced with gold winked at him from inside the leather bag, and Ryerson smiled. The bracelet was never far away these days. It symbolized the fantasy he and Virginia had found on Toralina.

With any luck, it would soon come to stand for the reality they were going to find here in Seattle. *With any luck?* Hell, he'd been getting lucky since the night he'd found himself standing on Virginia's doorstep. He was on a roll. Nothing was going to stop him now.

VIRGINIA AWOKE about noon and knew for certain she was going to live to eat in another restaurant. She breathed deeply a few times and decided her stomach was almost back to normal. Even the headache had disappeared. She wriggled her toes and thought about a shower. The idea was enough to propel her out of bed.

Once on her feet, she found she wasn't quite as steady as she had thought, but other than that, she was in fair shape. She made her way down the hall to the bathroom, peeled off her nightgown and stepped under a hot spray.

The shower door opened a minute later, and Ryerson peered in with great interest. He examined her lush, wet curves, a faint smile in his eyes. "Does this mean you're ready for raw oysters and steak tartare?"

Virginia grinned. "Not quite. But I think I am going to be able to make the Andersons' party tomorrow evening. As far as today goes, though, I'd better stick with soup and crackers."

"You're in luck. That's one of my specialties. I assume all this interest in food means you're not coming down with the flu?"

Virginia shook her head quickly. "Nope. It must have been food poisoning."

"Well, don't look so pleased with yourself. You're not going anywhere," Ryerson warned darkly.

She stared at him. "What's that supposed to mean?"

"It means I'm keeping you here for another night."

He appeared very determined. Virginia had to admit the idea was not nearly as upsetting as it ought to have been. And it was, after all, the weekend.

"Why?" she asked cautiously.

"For observation," he said with a wicked grin. "Close observation."

Virginia was left staring at the shower door as he closed it firmly behind him. It was happening, she thought. Slowly, inevitably, she was becoming entangled in his life, and he was becoming entangled in hers. This was not the fantasy world of Toralina where she had felt like a different person. This was reality, and she had to face the fact that Ryerson was right. There was no way to conduct a safe, fantasy affair with him. The man was far too real to be treated like a dream lover.

She discovered that afternoon that it was very pleasant to be pampered by Ryerson. He went shopping in the Pike Place Market and brought home flowers along with the groceries. He prepared soup and served it with a flourish. He played checkers with her and allowed her to win twice. And that night he did not try to make love to her. Sensing that she was back to normal but still very tired from the ordeal, he simply held her close until she was sound asleep.

The whole experience gave Virginia an insight into just how comforting a passionate friendship could be. The question now, she knew, was whether to risk a live-in relationship. A part of her was still frightened of jeopardizing everything she was finding with Ryerson.

The next day was Sunday, and Virginia discovered that Ryerson's routine was almost identical to her own. They shared a lazy brunch together and then read the paper over a pot of tea while Mozart played softly in the background. It all felt very comfortable and very homey. Virginia began to imagine a string of such weekends extending into the future.

It just might work.

Ryerson sensed the wheels turning in Virginia's stubborn brain and smiled to himself. His luck was holding.

The Andersons' party was a crowded event held at the couple's Mercer Island home. The modern two-story house fronted Lake Washington. A spectacular garden led from the terrace down to the water where a private boat dock jutted out into the lake.

The house had been built for entertaining, and tonight it was filled with people. Virginia knew many of the guests because of her family's longtime presence in the Seattle business community. She introduced them to Ryerson, who, in turn, found himself readily accepted.

He also discovered that his relationship with Virginia was the source of much speculation. He should have anticipated that, he thought ruefully, as well as the veiled questions about Debby. The truth was, he'd been so involved in plotting to get Virginia into his life that he'd literally forgotten about his brief dating relationship with the younger Middlebrook sister. Funny how a little thing like that could slip a man's mind.

"Heard you were seeing one of the Middlebrook sisters," a balding, middle-aged man remarked confidentially to Ryerson as Virginia smiled across the room at someone and moved off through the crowd. "Thought it was the other one, though. The younger one. Must have been mistaken." He frowned, staring after Virginia. "What's the story? Are you two serious about each other or what? Name's Heatherington, by the way. Sam Heatherington. Known Ginny since she was a kid. She always was a nice girl. She'll make some man a good wife one of these days."

Ryerson's fingers tightened around the glass of Scotch he was holding. His eyes flicked to Virginia who looked poised and regal tonight in blue-green silk that was artfully draped around her magnificent figure. She looked sparkling and animated and utterly charming, her beautiful hazel eyes full of life. The perfect wife for a nice, respectable businessman such as himself, he thought with satisfaction. A lady on the surface, a passionate, adventurous lover underneath.

She was wearing the bracelet and Ryerson liked the way it gleamed on her wrist. He was coming to think of that bracelet as a substitute for a ring, he realized. Whenever he looked at it, he was vividly aware of the bond he was forging with Virginia. It annoyed him tonight that others didn't yet understand that bond, and it infuriated him that he had no way of explaining it.

Ryerson realized he was longing to be able to stake out his territory in the traditional ways, but so far he had no official claim on Virginia. Something within him seethed restlessly. He did not like living in this shadowy world between friendship and marriage. He turned to Sam Heatherington.

"I agree with you," he said smoothly, "Ginny is very nice. For the record the two of us have an understanding."

"Oho! Just good friends, eh?" The man winked knowingly. "Don't worry, I get the picture."

"Is that right?" Ryerson eyed him coolly.

"Sure," Heatherington said with a worldly air. "Can't say that I'm surprised. Everyone knows Ginny went through a terrible time with that bastard she married. I'll admit he had everyone fooled for a while, but ultimately it was obvious he was only after Middlebrook Power Systems." He glanced at the attractive older woman who was gliding up to stand beside him. "Isn't that right, dear? Ryerson, this is my wife, Anne. Anne, this is A. C. Ryerson, the man who bought out Middlebrook."

"How nice to meet you, Mr. Ryerson." Anne Heatherington smiled up at him, her eyes betraying her curiosity. "We've been friends of the Middlebrooks for years. My husband is right, you know. The only favor Jack Winthrop ever did Virginia was to kick the bucket. But he did a lot of damage to her before he finally made his exit. I said at the funeral that I doubted Ginny would ever marry again. I'm happy to see I might have been wrong."

Ryerson cleared his throat. This was getting more than a little annoying. But he was in no position, dammit, to claim he was marrying Ginny. Hell, he couldn't even claim she was living with him yet. "I was just telling your husband that Virginia and I are, uh, good friends. We have an understanding." Lord, what a weak way of phrasing it. He wanted to shake Ginny for putting him in this position.

Anne raised her eyebrows. "Is that right? An understanding? How do the Middlebrooks feel about their daughter being 'good friends' with the man who bought the family firm?"

"Why don't you ask the Middlebrooks that question?" Ryerson said through his teeth. He'd had enough. He turned around and plunged into the crowd, aware that his temper was on a short leash.

No one else proved quite as blunt as Anne Heatherington and her husband, but the curiosity and the questions were there in the eyes of several people who knew Virginia. As the evening wore on, Ryerson became increasingly frustrated and angry that he couldn't make his claim plain to one and all. Virginia herself seemed unfazed by the subtle curiosity around her, as far as Ryerson could tell, and that irritated him further.

As time passed, the leash on Ryerson's temper got shorter. Shortly after ten o'clock he glanced around the room, locating Virginia easily. She was half a head above most of the women guests, regal as a queen. And just as proud and stubborn as one, Ryerson told himself grimly. He finished his Scotch and started toward her with sudden determination.

Virginia saw him approaching and smiled happily. He looked so good, she thought with warm affection. Tall and strong and utterly virile. *A man a woman could trust to be there when the going got rough,* whispered a voice in her head.

"Hello, Ryerson," she said as he walked up beside her. "Enjoying yourself?"

"Not particularly. I've been too busy fielding questions about our so-called relationship."

"Oh, those questions." She laughed. "I've had a few myself. Everyone's very curious. First people can't figure out whether it was me or Debby they'd heard you were seeing, and then they want to know how serious we are."

"I hope you've been telling them we're very serious," Ryerson muttered meaningfully. He reached out and took the wineglass from her hand. "Let's go outside. I want to talk to you."

"Now?" She was startled. "Is something wrong?"

"Nothing that can't be fixed. Let's go." He took her hand and led her out of the crowded room onto the terrace. Then he started down into the garden.

The June evening was cool but not chilly. Virginia followed Ryerson willingly. It was a relief to take a short break from the party.

"Look at the city lights across the lake," she said chattily as they walked down toward the water's edge. "Aren't they beautiful tonight? So clear and sparkling. I haven't been in the Andersons' garden for quite some time. I'd forgotten how spectacular it is. Bill Anderson has made it a full-time hobby, you know. He's always putting in little ponds or exotic roses."

Ryerson ignored her running commentary. "I want to talk to you about us, Virginia."

She tensed. *Here it comes,* she thought. Ryerson's patience had finally run out. He was going to pin her down and extract an answer from her. "Do you think this is the time or the place, Ryerson?" she asked softly and knew she was instinctively stalling.

"I was planning to wait but I don't think I can," he said bluntly. He released her wrist, his fingers gliding over the bracelet. The moonlight was in his eyes as he looked down at her. "Everyone inside that house wants to know if we're going to get married. I'm not asking you that. I just want an answer to the question I asked you the other night. Will you come and live with me?"

Virginia hesitated an instant and then turned away from him and walked a few steps down a tiny, pebbled path. There was a pond at the end of the path. She reached out and touched a rose that was gilded with moonlight.

"Are you sure that's what you want, Ryerson?"

"I want you," he told her. "Not on a part-time commuting basis or for occasional weekends. I want you full-time."

Virginia took a deep breath. "I've been thinking about it," she began carefully.

"Hell." Ryerson's disgust was plain. "Going to wimp out on me, Ginny? Do you really think you can maintain a fantasy affair with me indefinitely? Do you think that I'll let you treat me that way?"

She frowned and swung around to face him. "Ryerson, listen to me. I told you I've been thinking seriously about the problem, and I have."

"It's not a problem, dammit, except in your mind!" He took two threatening paces toward her, his features grim in the shadows. "It's the logical next step in our relationship. I've had it with your shilly-shallying, Virginia Elizabeth!"

He was looming over her in the moonlight. Instinctively she backed up a pace and lifted her chin. "Don't shout at me. I'm trying to conduct a reasonable discussion here. After all, this is a major decision for both of us."

"*Reasonable.* You call your arguments *reasonable*? Your arguments against us living together are as dead as your former husband. Bury them all, lady—the arguments and him."

She was alarmed by his intensity. She took another step back out of his reach. "Please, Ryerson, this is a big move for me. I would appreciate it if you would—"

"If I would what? Give you some more time? Forget it. I want an answer and I want it now." He took another pace toward her.

Virginia lost her temper. "What the hell gives you the right to push me like this?"

"I'm not worrying about rights tonight. I'll push as hard as I have to in order to get an answer. Come on, you little coward, tell me you'll come and live with me."

"I am not a little coward!" she yelped just as her high-heeled sandal slipped on a mossy stone at the edge of the pond. "Furthermore, I am not . . . *Oh, no!*" She lost her balance and grabbed frantically for a nearby branch, which promptly snapped in her hand. A second later she toppled into the pond with a resounding splash.

"Virginia." Ryerson leaped to the edge of the pool and waded in after her, heedless of his shoes and expensive suit. "Dammit to hell, are you okay?"

Virginia spit out a lily pad and glared at him. "No, I am not okay. This water is freezing." She ignored his extended hand and struggled to her feet. Her dress was a sodden mass of clinging silk. "Now look what you've done."

"What *I've* done!" He stood knee-deep in the water and stared at her in outrage. "This isn't my fault. If you hadn't been such a wimp about answering my question, this wouldn't have happened."

"Is that right? Well, let me give you my side of the story," she hissed. "If you hadn't been so pushy and demanding, neither of us would be standing here soaking wet. You didn't even give me a chance to answer your stupid question in a civilized fashion."

"So what is the answer?" he roared.

"The answer is *yes.*"

Ryerson stared at her speechlessly for nearly thirty seconds. Eventually he found his voice. "You mean it? No more arguments? You'll live with me?"

"If I don't catch my death of pneumonia first," she retorted tartly.

"Ginny!" He caught her wet body close, his mouth warm and fierce against hers. "Ginny, honey, I swear you won't be sorry. It's going to work—you'll see."

She melted against him, her arms going around his neck. "If you say so, Ryerson."

"I say so." He kissed her again with rough urgency, and then he stepped back and gave her a charming, sexy, rather crooked grin. "Come on, let's go home. We've got the perfect excuse to leave. You're soaking wet." He took off his coat and slung it around her shivering shoulders.

She nodded quickly. "That's a fact. I'm freezing. We can sneak around the corner of the house without anyone seeing us."

"We're not sneaking anywhere," Ryerson declared. "We'll go back through the house and say a proper goodbye to our hosts."

"Ryerson! Are you serious? Look at me; I'm a mess. And you're wet up to your knees. What will people think?"

"That we're a couple of passionate lovers who tried to get in a quickie out in the garden and managed to fall into the pond instead."

Virginia laughed softly. "Don't be silly, Ryerson. No one's going to believe that. Neither one of us is the type."

"That's what you think. We're going to answer once and for all the questions they've been asking this evening. After this, no one's going to wonder whether we're serious about each other. They'll know."

An hour later, Virginia was snuggled once more in Ryerson's bed. He turned out the last of the bedroom lights and crawled in beside her. She eyed him with accusing eyes.

"You let them think the worst, Ryerson. You did it deliberately. I heard how you explained our little dunk in the pond to Mrs. Anderson. You made it sound as if I'd gotten so carried away with passion that I lost my balance, tumbled into the pool and pulled you in after me."

"Isn't that fairly close to the truth?" He smiled contentedly as he reached for her.

"It's not close at all. I wound up in that pond because we were arguing, not because we were making love."

"In a way we were making love," he informed her.

"How's that?"

He leaned over her, trapping one of her legs with his own. He framed her face with his forearms. "You were telling me you would take the risk of living with me. I consider that an act of love."

"*An act of love.*" The phrase hung in the air between them. Virginia tasted it on her tongue and knew Ryerson was hearing his own words echo in the room.

"*An act of love.*" The words had a variety of connotations. One of them was an euphemism for having sex. But there was another meaning, one that implied the emotions were truly involved. Until now, Virginia knew, she and Ryerson had both been very careful not to use the word *love* in any ambiguous sense. Now the four-letter word was smoking in the air between them.

"Don't panic," Ryerson said softly. "We're going to do very well together, you and I."

"Do you think so?" Ryerson didn't believe in love, she reminded herself. He was much too practical, too unromantic and too realistic to buy into such a fuzzy emotion.

"I'll stake money on it. The same way I staked money to win that bracelet."

Virginia smiled tremulously. "It's a little nerve-racking going through so many changes so quickly."

"We'll adjust."

"You're so confident."

He smiled. "Now that I've got you under my roof, I can afford to be confident." He bent his head and kissed her throat, his mouth warm on her skin.

"I can't believe we're the same two people who once calmly discussed a pleasant, undemanding little friendship that would require almost nothing from either of us." Virginia shivered delicately with passion as Ryerson found her breasts with his lips. She laced her fingers into his hair and held him close, lifting herself against his mouth.

"If it's any consolation," Ryerson said as he moved down her breasts to her soft stomach, "I don't think we are the same two people."

"What happened to us?"

"I'm not sure. Has it occurred to you that we're changing in some ways, Ginny? That maybe Toralina wasn't just a fantasy world that we stepped into for a while and then left behind? Maybe we're not quite the same two people we were before we went down there."

She sucked in her breath as his fingers moved persuasively on the inside of her thighs. "Yes," she whispered. "It's occurred to me." Then she giggled in delight. "And judging from the expressions on the faces of the Andersons' guests tonight when we came back in from the garden, I think it's occurred to a few other people, too."

Ryerson laughed softly and began to stroke her tenderly. Deliberately he sought out the warm, damp, hidden places that he had claimed before. Virginia curled into him, twining one leg around his strong thigh. She touched him as intimately as he was touching her, glorying in the near-violent response she called forth.

Ryerson drew out the lovemaking, teasing and tormenting his passionate victim until she cried out for release.

"Soon," he promised over and over. "Soon."

"Now," Virginia pleaded, clutching at him. "I want you so. I need you."

"Tell me exactly what you need."

Virginia clung to his shoulders and wrapped her legs around his waist while she whispered the words in his ear. In a soft, seductive voice she made the plea as graphic as possible, and she knew her throaty descriptions of what she wanted nearly sent Ryerson over the edge. He shuddered in her grasp.

"Oh, Ginny," he muttered hoarsely. "Sweet Ginny. You're going to drive me out of my mind."

"Tell me exactly how you want me to do it."

Ryerson did exactly that.

The next afternoon after work, they took the ferry to the island where Virginia's cottage was located. Ryerson had it all planned, as usual. He explained everything to Virginia as he parked his Mercedes in the driveway and walked her to the front door of her home.

"We'll pack your clothes and whatever else we can get into your car, and I'll have a mover come in and do the rest. We can send some of your things over to my island place. It could use some furniture. I've always kept it pretty bare." He turned the key in the lock of her door.

"Maybe I shouldn't give up the lease on this place," Virginia said hesitantly. It was still hard to believe in a long-term future.

"You won't be moving back here anytime soon," Ryerson said harshly as he pushed open the door. "So don't worry about the lease. Let it expire."

Virginia started to say something else, but the words died as she stepped through the front door and confronted the shambles that awaited her.

"Oh, my God," she breathed as she surveyed the chaos in her front room. "I've been burglarized."

EIGHT

"How dared they do this to me? How dared they? They had no right to come in here and tear this place up. I'm going to put traps in the front yard. I'll get a huge dog. I'll get a gun. Yes, that's exactly what I'll do. I'll buy a gun. If they ever come back, I'll be ready for them." Virginia stormed back and forth across the living room, picking up magazines, shoving things back into their proper drawers and righting the furniture with furious energy.

"Calm down, Ginny." It wasn't the first time Ryerson had tried to soothe her. He had been saying "Calm down" and "Take it easy" on an average of every two minutes since the police had left. That had been over an hour ago.

"I mean it, Ryerson. I really am going to get a gun."

"You are not going to get a gun, Ms Amazon," he told her. "You're going to come and live with me, instead— remember? You won't have to worry about anyone coming back here, because you won't be living here."

He examined a pillow that had been ripped open with a knife. The stuffing was scattered all over the rug. His hand clenched in silent fury, but he kept his voice calm.

Virginia glared at him. "I'm not so sure about moving in with you now. I don't want whoever did this to think he can scare me off."

Ryerson's expression turned stony. He tossed aside the pillow and walked over to close his big hands around Virginia's shoulders. "Ginny, you are not the brave widow lady trying to hold the farm against a bunch of gunslingers sent over from the neighboring ranch. The local kingpin is not after your property. You rent this place, remember? The police said this was an act of vandalism, pure and simple. I know you're angry and you've got a right to be. But you're going to stay rational."

"Meaning I'm supposed to just pack up and move out of here?" She glanced around at the mess the invaders had made. A desire for revenge was burning in her. The knowledge that she would probably never get it was enraging.

"Right." Ryerson released her and took the stack of magazines from her hands. "We're going to put this place back into some semblance of order, and then we're going to pack your suitcases and get you out of here."

"I don't know, Ryerson," she said fretfully. "Maybe I ought to stay here a night or two. After all, whoever it was might come back."

"And you want to be here when he does?" Ryerson asked incredulously. "Don't be a fool, Ginny. You don't have a gun, you don't have a big dog and you don't have any booby traps for the front yard."

Virginia thought about that. "You could stay here with me."

"I could, but I'm not going to. Neither of us is going to spend the night here. We've already agreed that you would move in with me, and that's the way it's going to be. Why don't you start packing?"

She turned reluctantly. She was still simmering with outrage, and she knew that was probably having an effect on her thinking processes. Maybe Ryerson was right, but she didn't like admitting it.

"I really am going to get a gun," she mumbled as she started down the hall.

"No, you are not going to get a gun."

"That's what you think." Virginia scowled at him over her shoulder. "I'm going to buy a gun, and I'm going to learn how to use it."

Ryerson sighed. "Virginia, you know the statistics as well as I do. If you did get a gun and if you did have occasion to use it, odds are you'd either get shot yourself or you'd kill some innocent victim and have to live with that fact the rest of your life. What if it was a couple of little kids who did this? What if they had broken in and found the gun in the course of tearing this place up? They could have used it on themselves or one of their playmates. That's a far more likely scenario than you shooting it out with the bad guys."

"It's the principle of the thing!"

"Don't you think I know that? That doesn't change things. You're not getting a gun."

"You can't stop me!"

"I can and I will," he retorted with icy calm.

"What have you got against a woman defending herself?" Virginia demanded furiously.

"Nothing. But you're not going to do it with a gun."

His implacable attitude infuriated her. "That's what you think," she said.

He swung around with such suddenness that Virginia gasped and stepped back.

"Ryerson?" she whispered, not understanding the cold grimness in his eyes.

He walked toward her until he was standing directly in front of her. "No guns," he said distinctly. "Got that? You know nothing about them, and you can't possibly learn enough in a few days to make yourself an expert. Which is what you would need to be to handle an intruder. Hell, even experts screw up. That scenario I just painted for you? The one where an innocent person gets shot? I didn't just borrow that from an antigun ad."

Her eyes widened as she realized how serious he was. "What is it?" Virginia whispered. "What happened?"

"My father was an expert, Ginny. He kept guns in the house and he made sure my brother and I learned how to use them. He said it was safe to have weapons in the house as long as everyone knew how to use them and respected them. Then one night my kid brother, who had been out on a late date, tried to sneak back in without waking anyone. But he didn't quite make it. Dad heard a noise in the hall."

Virginia closed her eyes, aware of what was coming. "Oh, Ryerson."

"Yeah. Dad shot him, thinking he was an intruder. Jeremy lived, but it was a miracle. Dad never did forgive himself. The next day he got rid of every gun he had ever collected."

"How terrible for your family."

"It was. No guns, Virginia."

It was useless arguing with him, Virginia decided. Exasperated, but considerably subdued by the grim tale he had just related, she started back down the hall.

"What I don't understand is why they didn't steal anything," she muttered. "They just trashed the place. And why me? Do you realize this is the second time someone's broken into a place where I've been staying? There was that prowler down on Toralina the night before we left the island and now this. It's not fair."

"Yeah. I know."

Something in his too-quiet tone stopped Virginia. There was a long silence as she stood there in the hall, thinking. Intuitively, she knew Ryerson was doing exactly the same thing. Slowly she turned around and stalked back toward the living room. Ryerson was standing where she had left him, the newspapers in his hands.

"You don't really think there could possibly be . . . ?" Virginia let the sentence trail off.

"Any connection? No. It's too unlikely. Too bizarre. Toralina is a couple of thousand miles away. And that guy down there was no vandal. He was definitely a hotel prowler looking for valuables." But Ryerson kept watching her with a thoughtful, hooded gaze.

Virginia licked her lips. "Whoever did this might have been looking for valuables, too. He might have done a messier job of it this time because he figured he had the place to himself and he could be more thorough."

"But nothing was taken," Ryerson pointed out softly.

"True. Maybe he didn't find what he was looking for."

"Virginia, you're letting your imagination run away with you. There couldn't be any connection between the two crimes. That would imply that someone followed us all the way from Toralina. Highly unlikely. Why choose us to follow home? There were people staying in that resort who were a lot wealthier than we are."

Virginia sat down slowly on the arm of the sofa. She clasped her hands and put them between her knees. "The bracelet."

Ryerson betrayed no evidence of surprise, and she knew at once the same thought had been drifting through his mind. He put down the newspapers and sat down in the overstuffed armchair. He stretched out his legs and regarded the toes of his large, sturdy wingtips. "As far as we know, the only one who knows we have the bracelet is Harry Brigman."

"Maybe he wants it back. Perhaps it really was a family heirloom, one that he had no right to lose in a card game. Maybe it's more valuable than we realize."

"Or maybe he just doesn't like losing at poker." Ryerson put his elbows on the arms of his chair and rested his chin on laced fingers. His silver eyes fastened on her. "You do realize we're really reaching here, don't you? The odds are the incident on Toralina was exactly what it appeared to be: a hotel prowler. Happens all the time in the best hotels."

Virginia nodded glumly. "To tell you the truth, I don't really want to think there is a connection. It's too scary."

"There is one thing we could do that would instantly relieve our minds," Ryerson said after a moment.

Virginia looked up quickly. "What's that?"

"I could contact the Toralina police and find out if the prowler was ever picked up. If by chance they caught someone and he's been in jail all this time, we could be certain that whoever broke in here was not the same person."

Virginia brightened. "Great idea. Let's do it."

Ryerson surged up out of the chair. "Okay. I'll take care of it tomorrow. In the meantime, let's get this place put back together. It's getting late and we've got a ferry to catch."

"Ryerson, if there is some connection between what happened here and what happened on Toralina, I might have to seriously consider getting a gun," Virginia said quietly.

Ryerson lost his patience. He put a firm palm on Virginia's nape and propelled her down the hall to the bedroom. "For the last time, you are not getting a gun. Guns are dangerous. Innocent people get killed with guns. Forget the whole idea. Now pack."

"Ryerson, if you're serious about living with me on a full-time basis, I think I ought to warn you that I've been on my own for a long time. I don't take orders well."

"If you're serious about living with me on a full-time basis, you ought to know that I don't respond well to veiled threats and muttered warnings," he told her cheerfully. "Go pack."

Virginia was at her desk two days later when her sister phoned and invited her to lunch.

"Is this a genuine invitation, or are we going to split the check?" Virginia asked.

"This is an honest invitation," Debby assured her. "I thought we'd celebrate your surrender."

"My *what*?"

Debby laughed on the other end of the line. "I talked to Mom last night. She said you had just called to give her your new address."

Virginia tapped a pencil on her desk. "How is everyone taking the news? Mom sounded a little taken aback on the phone, but she didn't say too much except, 'Oh, I see.'"

"She's torn between delight that you've finally decided to give another man a chance and shock that you're moving in with the guy instead of marrying him. I told her that, knowing you, this was probably as close as she was going to get to having Ryerson as a son-in-law. She's still disgusted with me for failing to snag him, you know."

"Well, I trust she's not harboring any false hopes in my case. Ryerson and I are not getting married."

"That's what they all say in the beginning," Debby warned darkly. "Now, how about lunch?"

"I'll accept if you'll guarantee there will be no toasts to my so-called surrender."

"All right, but you're spoiling my fun."

Virginia hung up the phone with an uneasy feeling. But then, the word *marriage* always made her uneasy. She and Ryerson were living together, not getting married. Nothing had been said about marriage. This was an arrangement of two equals who happened to have a lot in common, including a mutual passion. She was not trapped and neither was Ryerson.

The uneasiness faded, and Virginia went back to work on the report in front of her.

Two hours later, she sat down across from Debby in a chic Pike Place Market restaurant that was crowded with business people and office workers. It was a warm, sunny day, and the jagged Olympic range was silhouetted against a brilliantly blue sky.

"Just imagine what a glitz-book writer could do with a situation like this," Debby said cheerfully. "Here we are, two sisters who have shared the same man. There should be great tension and high drama here. This has all the makings of a best-seller."

Virginia smiled, but she looked carefully into her sister's beautiful eyes. "Is there any cause for real tension and drama, Debby?"

"Nope. I'm glad I'm out of it, and I'm glad you're in. I think you and Ryerson make a perfect couple. By the way, in case you're wondering, we haven't exactly *shared* Ryerson."

Virginia buried her nose in the large menu. "I know," she mumbled.

"Oh, yeah?" Debby chuckled. "Ryerson made that clear right from the start, I'll bet."

"As a matter of fact, he did."

"He would. He's very blunt about things, isn't he? Well, it's the truth. To be honest, I found him a dead bore in that department, and I have to assume the feeling was mutual. Oh, he was attractive enough at first. He was different from the other men I've been dating. Bigger and stronger and tougher, somehow. Not just in size but in some other ways I can't explain. But I also found him intimidating on occasion. And when he wasn't being intimidating, he was a bit dull, I'm afraid. He always seems so solid and substantial. An immovable object, if you know what I mean. At least, I never found a way to move him. I never saw him get excited about anything. When I realized he wasn't even getting excited about the prospect of going away for a weekend, I knew we had a problem. Maybe there was just too much of a difference in our ages."

"Debby, I'm not sure we're required to discuss this in great detail. It's enough for me to know you're not pining for him."

"Ah, come on, Ginny," Debby retorted with great relish. "We're sisters. I love dissecting men. Great fun."

"Let's pick another man to dissect. Who are you seeing these days?"

"Tom Canter," Debby responded promptly. "He's a stockbroker. Made two hundred and fifty grand last year in commissions. He's hot. He also happens to love Sleaze Train."

Virginia glanced up from the menu. "Sleaze Train? Oh, yes, that hard-rock group that made Ryerson's ears ring for two days."

Debby grinned. "The man's taste in music is as boring as your own. What are you going to have for lunch?"

"The linguine with hot peppers and smoked salmon."

"Sounds good. I think I'll try the Cajun fish. With maybe a small salad."

Before Virginia could respond, a large shape moved between her and the window and a familiar male voice asked easily, "Mind if I join you?"

"Ryerson!" Virginia laughed up at him, aware of a frisson of pleasure at having run into him unexpectedly. He leaned down and gave her a proprietary kiss. "Sit down. You don't mind—do you, Debby?"

"Of course not. We've already finished talking about you, Ryerson. We're on another man now. Have a seat. What are you doing downtown? I see you've been shopping. Get anything exciting?" She noticed a paper sack he carried in one hand. The sack was emblazoned with the logo of a major downtown department store.

Ryerson shoved his purchase under his chair. "Nothing important. Just a small item I've been wanting to pick up." He reached for a menu. "I figured as long as I was downtown, I'd take Ginny to lunch." He glanced up. "But when I called your office, your secretary told me you were here having lunch with your sister."

"We're just about to order," Virginia said happily. "I'm glad you found us. You're in luck. Debby is picking up the tab."

Debby gave a dramatic gasp of dismay. "Hey, wait a second. I volunteered to take one other person to lunch, not two."

"Think of all the money I wasted on those Sleaze Train tickets," Ryerson pointed out, unperturbed. "You owe me."

"This, I will have you know, is a lunch designed to celebrate Ginny's new living arrangement," Debby told him loftily.

Ryerson grinned complacently. "Well, I'll have to admit I've already celebrated that a few times privately with Ginny. Okay, okay—I'll pay for my own lunch."

Virginia broke in before the conversation turned embarrassing. "If you two will kindly stop squabbling, we can put in our order and get back to work before quitting time." But inside she knew for certain she could relax. Whatever her sister might once have felt for Ryerson, it was over. Debby was treating him the way she would treat an older brother, and Ryerson was responding in kind.

They were finishing the meal when Ryerson spotted a business acquaintance across the room. "Have the waiter pour me another cup of coffee, will you, Ginny? I'm going to go say hello to Rawlins. My secretary tells me he's been trying to get hold of me all day."

The package under the chair crackled as he got to his feet. Virginia glanced at it with interest. Ryerson had made no mention of having to go shopping this morning when he had left the condo. She was the one who worked in the heart of the city. It would have been easy for her to pick up any small item he needed. She wondered why he hadn't asked her to do just that.

"So," Debby said as Ryerson moved out of earshot, "tell me the truth. Any chance the two of you might eventually get married?"

Virginia's pleasure at the unexpected luncheon faded. "That particular subject is not open for discussion, Deb. You know that."

"You're willing to live with the guy, but you won't marry him?"

"It's not an issue. Ryerson and I understand each other. Let's leave it at that."

"If you say so, but how does Ryerson feel about it? I don't think he sees himself as a trendy, fun-loving bachelor, which is just as well since he'd be a failure in that role. He's the type who wants to wallow in all the comforts of domestic bliss."

"I've told you, Ryerson understands. He's quite content the way things are, and so am I. Let's talk about something else, Deb."

"Dang. Older sisters never let younger sisters have any fun. If you ask me— Oops! Look out!"

Debby's exclamation came as the waiter who was bringing the coffee dodged to avoid a collision with a waitress carrying a tray of sizzling fish. The glass coffeepot in his hand tilted precariously and hot coffee slopped over the side.

"The package!" Virginia yelped as the coffee splashed down over the chair and threatened to splatter on Ryerson's purchase.

"I've got it," Debby announced. She leaned down quickly and scooped up the paper sack.

Unfortunately she grabbed the sack from the wrong end. The bag fell open as she yanked it out from under the chair.

A wickedly sexy, Ferrari-red teddy fluttered gracefully to the floor.

Virginia stared in shock at the silky scrap of lingerie. She wasn't the only one staring. Both the waiter and Debby were gazing at it, too. Debby's eyes flew to her sister's startled face, and she burst into giggles.

"Never in a million years would I have pegged A.C. Ryerson as the kind of man who would buy a sexy little teddy for his ladylove. Oh, Lord, Ginny, this is priceless. Utterly priceless."

The waiter wiped the chair and backed off with a hurried apology as Virginia leaned down to scoop up the red teddy. She was very much afraid her face was the same shade as the undergarment. But she was struggling to contain her own laughter, too.

Without any warning, Ryerson's large hand closed around the teddy a second before Virginia could reach it. The red silk appeared delicate and extremely fragile in his strong fingers. The sight made Virginia remember how tenderly Ryerson used his strength in bed and she blushed an even more vivid shade of crimson. Her eyes met his, and he smiled at her with sexy amusement.

Then Ryerson straightened and calmly thrust the lingerie back into the bag. Checking to make certain the coffee had been wiped off his chair, he sat down with the same aplomb he would have demonstrated at an annual meeting of Middlebrooks' board of directors.

"When the two of you have finished giggling, we can drink our coffee and leave." He glanced at the thin steel watch on his wrist. "It's getting late."

Virginia felt a wave of sisterly gratitude when Debby proved able, for once in her life, to keep her mouth shut. No one said another word about the red teddy until Ryerson kissed Virginia goodbye outside the entrance to her office building.

"I bought it for you to wear for me tonight. It's our anniversary, you know," he murmured in her ear.

"What anniversary?"

"It was a week and a half ago tonight that you and I seduced each other on Toralina."

"Oh." Virginia snatched the paper sack from his hand. "That anniversary. Since I get home before you, I'd better take it with me."

"Going to wear it to fix the margaritas?"

She smiled brilliantly. "Margaritas would be a nice touch, wouldn't they? Very appropriate." She nodded briskly and turned around to stride through the glass doors.

Ryerson watched her go, aware of the fact that he was aroused just thinking about seeing Ginny in the red scrap of lace and silk. She was going to look as sexy as hell. The bracelet would add a nice touch, too. He felt like the luckiest man on the face of the earth.

Whistling softly, he walked toward the Mercedes.

He was not whistling that evening when he strode into the condo after work. Ryerson was in a deadly serious mood, and when he realized that Virginia was not yet home, the concern he had been feeling transformed almost instantly into outright alarm.

"Ginny?" He called her name as he went hurriedly through the condo. She was always home ahead of him. Her office building was not that far away. She could walk the five blocks in ten minutes. He grabbed the phone and dialed her office. There was no answer.

Ryerson slammed down the receiver and paced to the windows. He stood staring out over Elliott Bay and told himself to calm down. She could have stopped at the state liquor store to get the ingredients for the margaritas, or she might have remembered an errand she hadn't recalled earlier when she'd said she'd be home before him.

He'd give her fifteen more minutes.

And then what, he wondered. He could hardly start calling the cops because Ginny was twenty minutes late getting home from work.

He switched on the answering machine to see if she had left a message. There was none. Ryerson glanced at his watch and picked up the phone again to call Debby. He punched out the number with short, vicious stabs. No answer.

Her parents' house.

He was dialing the Middlebrookses' number when he heard the key in the lock. Ryerson dropped the phone into its cradle and lunged for the door.

"Where the hell have you been?" he said through his teeth as Virginia swept into the hall with a load of packages. One of the sacks she was carrying was the one containing the red teddy.

She looked up, startled. "I just stopped off to pick up some dry cleaning. You're home a little early. What's wrong, Ryerson?"

"You're nearly half an hour late. You should have been here by the time I got home."

"I would have been, but at the last minute I remembered the cleaning. Ryerson, I don't see why you're so upset. There's plenty of time to change into the teddy and get the margaritas going."

"Forget the damned teddy," he grated. "From now on you let me know when you're going to be late. I want to know where you are every minute, is that clear? Leave a message on the answering machine or leave word at the office. Better yet, I want a daily schedule from you and you're to stick to it. No deviations."

"A schedule!" Virginia bristled. She set down her packages and turned to face him. "I think we'd better get something clear around here, Ryerson. I told you I am not accustomed to taking orders. I am also not in the habit of having to account for my every waking minute. If this is your idea of how a live-in arrangement is supposed to work, then you're laboring under a severe misapprehension. Who do you think you are to fly into a rage like this just because I'm a few minutes late getting home from work?"

He raked a hand through his hair and made a grab for his patience. He was hitting her like a ton of bricks and he knew it. But she did not yet know what he knew. "All right, calm down."

"I'm not the one who needs to calm down. You are. If I had known you were going to behave like this whenever I'm a little late, I would never have agreed to move in with you. We aren't married, Ryerson. Remember? And even if we were, I wouldn't tolerate this kind of treatment. I put up with enough garbage from my husband to last a lifetime. I will never allow another man to jump on me with both feet."

She was getting hysterical, he thought and it was his own damned fault. He *had* jumped all over her. He held up a hand. "Take it easy. Let me explain."

"I will not take it easy. I'm angry. You have absolutely no business yelling at me like this. I won't let you get away with it. I won't let you do this to me. *You have no right.*"

"I have all the right in the world," he retorted. "I've been going out of my mind waiting for you!"

"Because I was a few minutes late?" she asked in furious disbelief.

"No, not because you were a few minutes late!" he roared. "The reason I've been going crazy is that when I got back to my office this afternoon, there was a message from the Toralina police waiting for me. Somebody down there finally got off his rear and returned my call."

That stopped her in full flight. She looked at him, her mouth open. "From Toralina? A message about our prowler?"

"Not exactly," Ryerson said bluntly. "The Toralina cops didn't worry too much about our prowler after we left. They were too busy dealing with a homicide in one of the other suites."

"Somebody was murdered? Right there in the hotel?"

"Somebody we knew, Ginny. Harry Brigman. The guy who lost the bracelet to me in that card game. There is a possibility that the prowler in our room later that night was the murderer."

NINE

"I shouldn't have yelled at you the minute you walked in the door," Ryerson said quietly.

"Sure, but I'll let it go this time since there seem to have been mitigating circumstances," Virginia told him magnanimously. "Who knows? If the situation had been reversed, I might have done the same thing, given the same sort of provocation."

His mouth curved faintly. "You're very understanding."

"You can carry on with the apology later. Tell me everything you know about this mess," Virginia directed. She leaned her head back in the chair and peered up at him. The poor man really did look as if he'd been through a half hour of hell.

Ryerson began to pace the room in front of the windows, frowning. "I don't know all that much. Just enough to get worried. I gave you the gist of it. Shortly after we left the island, a maid found Brigman's body."

"You said you didn't think the prowler who got into our room was armed. If the man had just killed Brigman, wouldn't he have had a gun or something?"

"Or something. Brigman was killed with a knife. In the dark I could easily have missed seeing a knife."

"Oh." Virginia thought about that, and the thought sent little shivers down her spine. "And there you were running after him wearing nothing but your family jewels."

"Quality jewelry goes anywhere."

She smiled wryly. "Nevertheless, the whole thing is unsettling, isn't it?"

"That's putting it mildly. I don't like the outline. We meet a high-strung gambler who thinks he's riding high with Lady Luck. His luck runs out when he plays with me. He can't cover his gambling debts with cash, so he gives me the bracelet, instead. The next thing we know, he's dead and someone is searching our hotel suite. We leave the island in blissful ignorance, and a week after we get home, someone tears your cottage apart."

"You're wondering now if whoever ripped up my place really was looking for the bracelet?"

"The possibility has crossed my mind," Ryerson admitted. "I talked to the cops who handled your vandalism complaint. They agreed to check with the Toralina police and exchange information, but I'm not holding my breath. International police cooperation is more efficient in the movies than it is in real life. In real life, it involves a lot of paperwork, from what I understand."

"And cops, like most folks, probably hate paperwork."

"Probably. Besides, the general impression I got was that no one really thinks there could be any connection between what happened to your house and the murder on Toralina. Highly unlikely, I was told. The Toralina police said that as far as they could tell, Brigman was a loner who liked to island-hop in the Caribbean. He gambled heavily, but had no close friends or acquaintances."

"Did you tell the cops about the bracelet?" Virginia asked.

Ryerson hesitated. "I told the Toralina police I had won a piece of what appeared to be old jewelry from the murder victim. They didn't see any connection."

"In other words, no one really thinks someone followed us from Toralina just to retrieve the bracelet."

Ryerson shook his head. "You've got to admit, it doesn't sound very likely. How would this mysterious someone have even known we live here in Seattle? The logical assumption, Ginny, is that Brigman was killed by a hotel prowler who was just hunting randomly for valuables, and the vandalism at your place is an unconnected event."

"Agreed." Virginia took a deep breath. "All the same, I'm glad I'm living here with you right now instead of riding the ferry back to my cottage on the island. I don't think I'd enjoy being alone there tonight."

Ryerson stopped pacing. "I'm glad you're finding some positive aspects to this arrangement," he muttered.

Virginia smiled serenely. "Other than your jumping on me a few minutes ago because I came in a little late, it's been a pleasant experience."

Ryerson shot her a scowling glance. "A pleasant experience. Is that how you think of it? You're living with me, Ginny. That's not the same thing as checking into a motel for a few days, you know."

Her smile disappeared as she realized he was still annoyed. "I didn't say it was, Ryerson."

"*A pleasant experience.*" He shoved his hands into the back pocket of his slacks and stalked over to the window. "That's a hell of a way to describe it."

Virginia began to grow uneasy. Ryerson was not in his customary comfortable mood this evening. The man had had a rough day. "I didn't mean to offend you," she said quickly. "I just meant that things seem to be working out rather nicely. You know I had a few qualms at first. I wasn't sure I could live successfully with anyone again. I had grown to value my independence and my own space."

"But now that you've seen how generous I am with my closet space and my bathroom cabinets, you figure everything's going to work out, is that it? Just a couple of friends sharing an apartment and a bed. What do you think we are? Roommates?"

She straightened in the chair. "Ryerson, I understand that you're a little upset this evening, but there's no need to pick a fight with me."

"A little upset. The woman tells me she finds living with me a *pleasant* experience and then she wonders why I'm frothing at the mouth."

Virginia grinned in spite of herself. "Are you frothing at the mouth?"

He swung around. There was no answering humor in his silver eyes. "One of these days, lady, you're going to discover you can't have it both ways. You're either going to commit yourself to this relationship, in which case it won't matter if we're married or living together, or you're going to have to run for your life."

Her brief amusement vanished. She stared at him, shocked to the core. "What do you mean? Why would I have to run anywhere?"

"You'll have to run to escape me," he told her bluntly. "Because I'll be right behind you. Sooner or later I'll catch you, and when I do, you're going to find the courage to make a commitment. This roommate business sucks."

Virginia paled. "I didn't realize you were so unhappy in this relationship. I thought this was what you wanted."

"You want the whole truth? I'll give it to you. I'm tolerating our present arrangement because I see it as a stepping stone to marriage. Living with you is a whole heck of a lot better than not living with you. I am not unhappy, Virginia Elizabeth, merely impatient."

Her hands tightened on the arms of the chair. Carefully she pushed herself to her feet, aware of a dull anger. "I didn't realize you were thinking of marriage. I thought we understood each other. I already tried marriage once to a man who did not love me. It was a disaster. Why should I try it a second time?" Without waiting for a response she walked down the hall to the bedroom.

"Virginia."

She didn't pause, though she heard him storming down the hall behind her. Without a word, she slipped off her pumps and reached into the closet for a pair of jeans.

"Don't you dare draw any parallels between me and that fool you married," Ryerson grated from the doorway.

"I'm not drawing any parallels." She sighed as she stripped off her panty hose. "You're totally different, and I know that. But you don't love me."

"Is that right?" he roared sarcastically. "You think I'd go through all this nonsense for the sake of acquiring a roommate?"

Virginia looked up in astonishment. She stood holding the panty hose in one hand and her jeans in the other. "Ryerson, what are you saying?"

"I love you," he bit out, sounding not the least bit like a lover. "Do you hear me, lady?"

"Ryerson." She dropped the panty hose and jeans and ran to him. "I'm so glad. Because I love you, too. More than anything else in the world." She wrapped her arms around his waist and hugged him fiercely.

Ryerson's arms closed tightly around her. "Say that again," he ordered thickly.

"I love you. I've known that for several days now."

"Exactly how long have you known?"

She raised her head and saw the molten silver in his eyes. "Probably from the start, but most certainly since the night I fell into the Andersons' pond," she admitted with a small smile. "What about you? When did you first realize you might be falling in love?"

"The night you got sick all over my bathroom." He grinned down at her. "What a pair of wild, flaming romantics we are, huh?"

"I thought you didn't believe in love."

"I was a fool. I didn't believe in it because I hadn't ever experienced it. Once you've been knocked on your ass by it, though, you recognize it instantly."

"Oh, Ryerson." Virginia leaned into him, parting her lips for him, giving herself to him without words. She had always believed in the possibility of love. She just hadn't expected to find the courage within herself to take the risk again. Now that she had, she was slowly becoming aware of an amazing sense of freedom.

"What are you smiling about?" Ryerson asked against her lips.

"I was just enjoying the feeling of being free."

Ryerson held her fiercely and groaned. "Ginny, honey, you're not free. I thought you understood at last. There's no real freedom in this relationship of ours. We're both bound by a million strings, large and small, and the longer we're together, the more chains there will be between us. I want you badly, but I don't want you living here under an illusion."

She touched his nape with gentle fingers. "You're the one who doesn't understand, Ryerson. The freedom isn't in the relationship, it's in being able to choose the kind of relationship I want. I never thought I would be sufficiently free of the past to risk falling in love. But

I've discovered that I am free to make that kind of choice again. And I have chosen to fall in love. With you."

He kissed her again, hungrily, and eased her down onto the bed. Virginia was aware of his fingers on the fastener of her bra. Ryerson was whispering husky words of love and desire when an image flashed into Virginia's head.

"Ferris," she said starkly.

"What?" Ryerson smoothed the skin of her breast with his rough fingertips. He lifted his head and frowned down at her in puzzlement. It was obvious his mind was elsewhere.

"Dan Ferris," Virginia said slowly. "You said the Toralina cops told you Brigman had no close friends or acquaintances on the island, but he wasn't a total loner. He knew Dan Ferris. Remember the night we snuck back to our room after that swim in the ocean? We had to wait for Ferris and Brigman to get out of the way. They were arguing in the garden."

Ryerson sat up slowly. "Something about leaving the island. Ferris was getting restless. He told Brigman it was time to go. But Brigman refused."

"He and Brigman never gave any indication of knowing each other when they were both in the casino or at the restaurant," Virginia recalled. "And I never saw them sharing a drink. In fact, they acted like strangers every time we saw them together."

"Except the night we overheard them arguing in the garden," Ryerson concluded. "I wonder why they kept their association secret?"

"We can't be sure that they did. It might be that we just never saw them together except for that one evening."

Ryerson grew more thoughtful. "Ferris turned around on the path that night. He saw us."

"Which means he knows we saw him arguing with Brigman." Virginia clutched the front of her bra together and gazed up at Ryerson with troubled eyes. "You don't suppose he's the one who killed Brigman, do you?"

"They were arguing about leaving the island, not about the bracelet."

"True, but what if the part we heard was only a small piece of the argument? What if they had discussed something else more incriminating that night on the path? Ferris would have had no way of knowing how much we'd overheard."

"The one thing he could be sure of is that we were the only ones who could link him, even slightly, with Brigman," Ryerson said. He got to his feet.

"Where are you going?"

"I'm going to put in another call to the Toralina police. You might as well start dinner. This will take a while."

Virginia glanced down at her rumpled clothing. "I take it the big seduction scene is being postponed?"

Ryerson grinned from the doorway. "To be continued."

But Ryerson had other things on his mind after the phone call finally went through to Toralina.

"I don't like it," he told Virginia twenty minutes later. "They were very polite and agreed to check into Dan Ferris's background, but that was it. Ferris was just another tourist on the island, as far as they're concerned. He's long gone. They seem convinced, however, that the murderer was the hotel prowler and that Brigman probably interrupted him while the guy was going through Brigman's suite. After the murder, the prowler went on to the next likely looking hotel room."

"Which was ours?" Virginia started in on her scallops. "It's possible, isn't it?"

"Anything's possible, but you'd think the average prowler would be a little shaky after committing murder. Hard to picture him calmly going on with business as usual. It would take a real pro to be able to do that. After all, a prowler's specialty is sneaking around hotel rooms, not outright violence."

"But if it's true, it would mean there's no connection between what happened here and what happened down on Toralina. Which, in turn, would mean we're as safe as we ever were."

"I still don't like it." Ryerson pushed aside his plate and contemplated Virginia. "I think we're going to take another couple of days off."

Virginia looked at him. "But why? Where are we going?"

"To my place up in the San Juans. We'll take a long weekend. It will get us out of the city and it will give the Toralina police a couple of days to do some checking. Maybe by the time we get back, they'll have something. Can you get another couple of days off?"

"Yes. I still have some vacation time coming," Virginia said slowly. "You're really worried, aren't you, Ryerson?"

"If Ferris or someone else is after us or the bracelet, we're sitting ducks here in town. There are too many opportunities for him to make a move and get away with it. We'll be safer on the island. As far as anyone looking for us will know, we'll have dropped out of sight. Very few people know where my place is, and even if someone did locate it, the only way to reach it is by boat."

Virginia stirred uncertainly. "All right, I guess it won't hurt to disappear for a few days while the cops are checking things out. But what about the bracelet?"

"We'll wait until the banks open in the morning, and then we'll stick the thing in a safe-deposit box."

That night Ryerson double-checked all the locks before going to bed. When he walked into the bedroom, Virginia was sitting up against the pillows, waiting for him. She watched him undress and slide into bed beside her. Instead of reaching for her, however, he turned on his side and groped under the bed.

"What are you doing?" she asked.

"Just checking my insurance policy."

"You keep it under the bed?"

"Why not?" He settled back on the pillows and smiled at her. "There's a lot of unused storage room under a bed, you know. Now that I'm sharing this place with you, I have to find creative ways to use the available space."

"Ryerson," Virginia began very seriously.

"Maybe we should look for a bigger condo. If we had a two-bedroom place we could use the second room for storage."

"Ryerson," she tried again, leaning over him with a frown, "what have you got under the bed?"

"At the moment just a couple of suitcases and the insurance stuff I told you about. But if we got one of those special storage lockers designed to fit under a bed, we could store all kinds of junk."

Virginia planted her palms on his chest and glared at him ferociously. "You've got a gun under there, don't you?"

He wrapped his fingers around her wrists. "Don't be silly," he told her roughly. "You know how I feel about guns. Come here and tell me again how much you love me." He pulled her down on top of him and silenced her muffled protests with a kiss. No need to tell her he'd bought the damned gun the morning after they'd found her cottage ransacked.

Virginia and Ryerson were at the bank when it opened the next day. Ryerson's Mercedes was already packed, and they were ready for the trip to the San Juans. He was impatient to be on his way. Virginia had been aware of his restlessness all morning. His mood would not have been very obvious to someone who did not know him well, however. Even when he was at his most volatile, Ryerson still appeared controlled and contained. But Virginia was coming to know him very well. The appearance of self-control concealed an alert readiness that reminded her of a hunting animal that senses prey but has not yet spotted it.

"Sign here, Virginia," Ryerson said briskly. "I want your name on the access form. The bracelet is half yours."

Obediently Virginia picked up the pen. She had her name half scrawled on the signature line when something stopped her. "Ryerson?"

"What, honey?"

"I don't want to put the bracelet in the vault."

He glanced at her in surprise. "Why not? It will be safe there. One less thing for us to worry about."

She shook her head, suddenly sure of herself. "I'd rather keep it with us."

"But, Ginny . . ."

"Please, Ryerson. Let's keep it with us." She put a hand on his sleeve. "I know it seems logical to store it here, but I just have this feeling we should take it with us."

He looked down into her anxious eyes and hesitated. "Ginny, it will be safe here."

"I know. But I want it with us." She had to convince him, she realized. It was crucial, though she had no idea why she was so sure of that. "Please, Ryerson. Humor me. If we're in danger, it won't matter if we have the bracelet with us. Whoever's after it will assume we have it, anyway."

"Dammit, Ginny, it doesn't make any sense to drag this thing around with us."

"You've got your insurance policy. This is mine." She dropped the bracelet into her purse.

Ryerson groaned in resignation. "The hell with it. If that's the way you want it, I'm not going to argue. We've wasted enough time as it is. Let's get out of here."

He wasn't pleased, Virginia realized as she followed him out to the car. She waited out his mood in silence, letting him concentrate on getting them clear of downtown traffic. When they were finally on Interstate 5, heading north toward the ferry docks that serviced the islands scattered from Seattle to Canada, she broke the taut silence.

"I can't explain it, Ryerson. This morning I agreed with you about putting the bracelet into the vault. But at the last minute I got this overwhelming feeling we should keep it with us."

"Save me from a woman's logic," he muttered.

"Well, I happen to be a woman!"

He shot her an unreadable glance. "I'm not arguing that."

Silence settled down on the Mercedes once more. Virginia decided Ryerson was brooding. Neither one of them said more than a few words until they were on board the ferry that would take them on the first leg of their journey. Then Virginia tried to reopen communication.

"Will this ferry take us to the island where you have your vacation place?"

Ryerson leaned against the rail, watching the islands, large and small, float past the ferry. "No. We'll get off at the next stop. I keep a boat in a marina there. We'll use the boat to get to my place."

"Are you going to spend the whole weekend glaring at me?" Virginia asked.

Ryerson turned his head in surprise. "Is that what I was doing? Glaring at you?"

"When you're not actively brooding about my lack of common sense."

He gazed at her for a long moment. "Do you want to know what I was thinking about, Ginny?"

"If you want to tell me."

"I was thinking that I've been behaving a lot like a husband instead of a lover during the past couple of days."

She flicked him a quick glance. "I see."

"I doubt it. In case you haven't noticed, I sometimes have trouble playing fantasy man. I lost my temper with you yesterday, and I got annoyed with you again this morning. I can't guarantee it won't happen again. I wasn't cut out to be a dream lover."

"You did a good job on Toralina," she couldn't resist pointing out.

"Is that why you think you're in love with me? Because of the way I treated you while we were on Toralina? If so, Ginny, you're setting us both up for a fall."

"I don't think I'm in love with you. I know I'm in love with you. I can handle the real you, Ryerson."

"Even when I come off sounding like an irate husband?"

"The real question is, can you handle me when I sound like a shrewish fishwife?"

Ryerson's smile was his first in hours. He put his hands behind her neck and slowly, inevitably, drew her close. "I can handle you, regardless of what kind of wife you turn out to be."

She looked up at him, trying to determine if he was teasing her. There was no sign of it. She moved in his arms and decided the safest thing to do was to ignore the reference to wife. After all, she had inadvertently brought the word into the discussion.

Two hours later, Ryerson guided his small cruiser into a tiny, secluded cove on the east side of what appeared to be a deserted island. Virginia stood in the stern, watching with interest as he tied the boat up at a private dock. There was a small boathouse attached to the planked dock. Both were designed to float on the tide. Nestled in the trees several yards above the shoreline was a cabin.

"Does anyone else live on the island?" she asked. "It looks uninhabited except for your place."

"There are a couple of other vacation cottages on the opposite side. The owners rarely use them. For all intents and purposes, I've got the whole island to myself." Ryerson began unloading the suitcases and packages they had brought with them. "It's a little primitive, Ginny. I didn't build the place to be a love nest."

"No mirrored ceilings or red velvet wallpaper?"

"Afraid not. Also no phone and no dishwasher. Disappointed?"

"That depends. What about hot water and electricity?"

He gave her an offended look. "Honey, I'm a man who knows power systems, remember? Don't worry.

You'll have hot water and electricity. Also a stereo. Just as soon as I get the generator started."

Virginia smiled cheerfully. "In that case, I'm a contented woman."

The small cabin was cold and damp from having been closed for months, but the atmosphere changed after Ryerson spent several minutes out back with the generator that supplied power to the cottage. When he had finished with that, he started a fire in the stone fireplace. By the time he had the blaze going, Virginia had his Scotch poured and dinner on the stove.

"Perfect," she mused as she sat down beside him on the old sofa after the meal had been served. "Brings back fond memories of our first meeting. The only thing missing is the storm and Mozart."

"You're not going to have to wait long for either," Ryerson told her as he fished a compact disc out of its plastic storage container and put it on the player. He glanced out the window. "The rain is starting already."

"Ah, that's a nice touch," Virginia murmured, sipping her wine.

"I special-ordered the storm." Ryerson settled back down beside her as the strains of a violin concerto filled the room. He smiled slowly as he picked up his glass of cognac. "You know something? I had a hell of a hard time getting to sleep that night in your cottage. All I could think about was how nice it would be to wander down the hall and crawl into bed with you. I knew then I was in serious trouble."

"You weren't the only one," she confessed. She leaned her head against his shoulder. "I just wish we were here tonight because we really had decided to take a long weekend, not because we're trying to lie low while the Toralina police come up with some answers."

"I know," Ryerson said quietly, his tone hardening. "This is only a temporary hideout, at best. We sure as hell can't stay here indefinitely. But I don't like the idea of you being vulnerable in the city. It's too hard to keep an eye on you there. Any creep could snatch you off the street."

"The Toralina cops are probably right. There's no real reason to think there's a connection between Brigman's death and the bracelet. I'll bet no one even knew he had the bracelet."

"Ferris could have known. That's what worries me. If he knew about the bracelet, he might also know how Brigman lost it."

There was no real argument on that score. Virginia sighed and finished her cognac. Then she smiled a secret smile and got to her feet. "Stay where you are, Ryerson."

"Where are you going?"

"I'm going to get ready for bed."

"I'll help you," he volunteered with an expression of lazy lechery in his eyes.

"Not at this stage. Just wait right where you are."

She went down the hall to the bedroom and closed the door behind her. Then she quickly opened her suitcase and drew out the scandalous red teddy she had secretly packed. Eyes alight with sexy mischief, she undressed and slipped into the sensual concoction.

When she was finished, she stood in front of the small mirror and tried to determine the effect.

The teddy was nothing but a cobweb of silk and lace. It concealed very little of her ripe figure. Virginia faltered slightly in her resolve. This style in underwear was still new to her. What she needed was something to give her the confidence it would take to sashay out into the living room. She opened her purse and took out the bracelet.

When she had the emeralds clasped around her wrist, Virginia felt much bolder. She took a deep breath, opened the door and strode down the hall.

Ryerson was down on one knee, fiddling with the fire, when she arrived in the doorway behind him. He glanced over his shoulder and his eyes burned brighter than the flames on the hearth when he saw her.

"Come here," he murmured softly as he replaced the iron poker. He didn't move.

Virginia went slowly toward him, excitement and love and a glorious sense of abandon leaping in her veins. "Debby said she thought you were just about the last man on earth who would buy something like this for a woman," she whispered, "but you know something, Ryerson?"

"What?" He reached up and tugged her down onto the rug beside him. His fingers slid beneath the silk strap of the teddy. He seemed fascinated with it.

"I wasn't surprised at all when this thing fell out of the sack at the restaurant." She laughed up at him with her eyes. "Somehow it seemed exactly like something you might buy on a whim."

He grinned, stretching out beside her. He watched the way the firelight played on her skin. "It's the first time I've ever been struck by that particular whim. Do you have any idea how much nerve it takes to walk up to a lingerie counter and ask for something like this? Greater love hath no man." He slid the straps of the teddy down over her shoulders so that the lace was barely cupping her breasts.

Virginia put her arms around his neck and drew him down to her. "Maybe one of these days I'll find the guts to buy you a pair of those itty-bitty black bikini briefs they make for men."

"Don't bother," he advised. "I've got some limits." He eased the teddy slowly down to her hips, his fingers gliding over her breasts with obvious pleasure. "Tell me again that you love me, Ginny."

So she told him. Again and again, she told him as he stripped the teddy off her completely and opened her to his touch.

He rewarded her with tantalizing, seductive caresses that made the secret parts of her blossom. When he bent his head and kissed the dew from the petals, Virginia clung to him, crying out her release in his arms. He held her as she shivered delicately.

"I love you, Ginny."

She looked up at him as he loomed over her. The truth of that statement was in his eyes as he sheathed himself tightly within her.

TEN

Ryerson slid out of bed much later that night and turned to look at the sleeping woman on the bed. They had both been exhausted from making love, but he hadn't been able to sleep since he had carried Virginia into the bedroom. That had been over two hours ago. It was after midnight now.

There was a strange restlessness driving him tonight. He had experienced it before around Ginny, and he knew how to ease it temporarily. All he had to do was go back to the bed and make love to her until she awoke and welcomed him into her soft, hot warmth. Sheathed within her with her silken legs wrapped around his thighs, he could ignore everything but the glorious sensation of losing himself in her. The wonder of possessing her and being possessed by her would wipe the restlessness from his mind for a time. He was a simple creature at heart, he decided wryly. Sex with Ginny satisfied him as nothing else ever had.

But it was not enough. Reluctantly he turned away from the bed and went out into the hall, scooping up his jeans as an afterthought. The cabin was cold.

Out in the living room, Ryerson pulled on the jeans. The fire had started to die hours ago, and he had not turned on any auxiliary heat. Outside, the rain was still falling with a soft, steady beat. It wasn't a particularly heavy rain, just a light, continuous drizzle. A typical Northwest rain.

Ryerson didn't bother with a light. He didn't want to wake Ginny. In any event, he knew his way around well enough to get by with the glow from the embers on the hearth. He remembered leaving the cognac bottle on the low table beside the sofa. A little fumbling recovered the glass he had set aside earlier. He poured a shot of cognac and moved to the window that overlooked the cove.

The sky was a slightly different shade in the distance. The rain was going to end soon. A watery moon was already trying to squeeze through the clouds. There was enough of a glow to see the cruiser bobbing in the water down at the dock. Ryerson sipped the cognac and watched the boat, remembering how Ginny had looked earlier that afternoon when she had sat in the stern, her seal-brown hair whipping around her expressive face.

Virginia was the first woman he had brought to the island, the first one he had ever really wanted to bring here. This place had always been his private retreat. Then he pictured Ginny as she had been a couple of hours ago, trembling in his arms. When he brought her sexual release, he felt like a conquering hero, master of all he surveyed and most important, master of Virginia Elizabeth Middlebrook. He gloried in his own manhood when she experienced the full potential of her femininity.

When she brought him release, he knew a satisfaction and peace that went to his soul.

He understood now why the primitive side of a man tended to get possessive when the right woman walked into his life.

Ryerson knew he needed Ginny. He acknowledged in that moment that he would do anything to keep her. He stood at the window and looked out at the cove and admitted the truth to himself. He needed her and wanted her as he had never needed or wanted anyone before in his life. He had to find a way to tie her more securely to him. He did not trust the bonds of a live-in relationship. He was damned if he would be roommates with the woman he loved.

The words hovered in his mind like a hawk. Words of great power; words he had always avoided. Words he had never really understood until he had met Ginny.

He had reveled in hearing her confess her love for him today, but it was still not enough. He was a greedy man. He loved her too much to want her as his roommate. He wanted her as his wife. He wanted her bound to him with all the chains modern civilization could provide.

Which put him squarely between a rock and a hard place.

If he truly loved Ginny, he could not force her into marriage. Her fear of the institution ran deep, and he had to respect that fear. He loved her too much to push her into something that genuinely terrified her.

But he loved her too much to be content for long with having her for a live-in lover. A primitive part of him had surrendered to an ancient need. He needed to know that the woman he loved belonged to him in every way possible. He sensed that as long as she feared marriage to him, she was, on some level, fearing a complete relationship with him. And that knowledge scared Ryerson.

There was a part of her that still did not belong to him.

The problem was going to eat him alive, night and day. Ryerson took another swallow of cognac and wondered how long he would be able to tolerate the torment. Perhaps he could learn to live with it. After all, he would have Ginny in his bed and in his life. What more could a man want?

A lot more, Ryerson knew. He swore softly. The truth was, he would never be certain of her until she was ready to take the risk of marrying him. The fact that she could still resist marriage left him with a queasy, sinking feeling.

Ryerson swirled the cognac in his glass and narrowed his eyes as he absently watched the small boat in the cove.

"Ryerson?"

Virginia's soft, questioning voice brought him out of his reverie. He turned his head and smiled slightly. She looked soft and sexy and infinitely desirable standing there in the shadows in her prim terry-cloth robe. He had removed the teddy a long time ago, and she had never put it back on. Her hair was tousled and her feet were bare. She had forgotten to take off the bracelet, he saw. Her arm moved and the gems danced in the shadows.

"What are you doing up?" Ryerson asked, holding out his hand.

She came toward him, stepping into the circle of his embrace. "I woke up and you were gone."

"And that bothered you?"

"Yes."

He tightened his arm around her. "You should know by now that I'm never going to be very far away."

She was silent for a moment. "I know."

"I love you, Ginny. I'll try not to push you anymore. I won't drag you to the altar. I don't want to force you into something that scares you as much as marriage does. We'll do things your way."

She put her arms around his neck and softly kissed his throat. "Thank you, Ryerson. Thank you for everything."

"Don't thank me. I don't have any choice in the matter," he muttered, inhaling the scent of her hair. "I want you to be happy with me, Ginny. I don't want you climbing walls, looking for a way out or living in fear of being trapped."

"I am happy."

"That's all that matters for now." He caught her hair in his fingers and made a fist. Gently he used the grip to arch her head back so that he could kiss her. He heard her gentle sigh and felt the firm curves of her breasts beneath the robe. The terry cloth parted of its own accord, and Ryerson found himself gazing down into deep, sensual shadows.

He was about to slip his hand inside the open robe and explore the mysteries he knew awaited him when he saw another kind of shadow out of the corner of his eye. This one was moving down in the cove near the boat. Ryerson froze.

"What's wrong?" Instantly Virginia sensed the change in him. She looked up anxiously.

"Something moved down by the boat."

"An animal?"

"Possibly. But I think it's one with two feet instead of four." He released her and moved closer to the window, trying to peer through the darkness. The shadow flickered again, moving onto the dock and heading toward the boat. Ryerson swung around, grasping Virginia roughly by her forearms.

"Listen to me. I want you to stay right here and keep everything locked up tight. I'm going down to the boat."

"I'll go with you," she said immediately.

"No you will not." He released her and moved quickly down the hall to the bedroom. He thrust his feet into sneakers and reached under the bed for the .38.

Virginia was waiting for him in the other room, her expression taut and anxious. She looked at the weapon in his hand and her mouth tightened. "Ryerson, I don't think you should go down there."

"I don't have much choice. I can hardly call the cops. There aren't any on the island. Dammit, I thought we'd be safe here." He was already at the back door, letting himself out into the soft rain. He paused only to glance back briefly. "Remember what I said, Ginny. Stay inside and keep everything locked up tight."

"Ryerson, please . . ."

He gave her no further chance to argue. Closing the door softly behind him, he waited only until he heard her slide the bolt in place. Then he made his way around the corner of the cabin, heading for the cover of the trees.

His main advantage, Ryerson decided, was that he knew his way around the island. He did not need to follow the path from the cabin to the dock.

The rain silenced his movements through the woods. Ryerson avoided the impregnable blackberry thickets and made his way around the larger depressions in the ground, which he knew would be holding rainwater.

He could keep an eye on the path from his position in the trees, and so far no one was moving toward the cabin. That meant whoever was messing around with the boat was still busy at the dock. He tried to imagine who would be attempting to steal the small cruiser and came up with no viable prospects. Then he started wondering who might want to wreck the boat. That led to more interesting speculation.

Dan Ferris's name came to mind.

Somehow, Ryerson knew, this was all connected to that damned bracelet. Every instinct he possessed was convinced of that.

A stand of pine provided concealment near the dock. Ryerson used the trees and the darkness for cover as he moved toward the boathouse. In another moment, he would have to step out into the open. He hoped the rain would continue to obliterate any noise he might make. He was no *ninja* warrior, that was for sure—just a man who knew motors and power systems inside out. Hardly the kind of background needed for this type of thing. The gun weighed a ton in his hand. He hadn't used one after the night his father had accidentally shot Jeremy, except for his brief stint in the army.

Ryerson was about to take his chances in the open when the shadow inside the cruiser moved abruptly. A man stepped out onto the dock. Ryerson held his breath and tried to relax his grip on the gun. If this was going to work, he had to look cool and in command. No worse than facing a board of directors or an angry client, he told himself reassuringly.

But before he could move, the man on the dock opened the metal door of the boathouse and went inside. The door stayed open. Ryerson released the breath he had been holding and moved silently across wet pine needles to the side of the small building.

This was a chance he couldn't pass up. If he could reach the door in time he could slam it shut and lock it from the outside, effectively trapping the intruder in the boathouse.

He raised the gun and leaped lightly onto the dock. He was only a foot from the open door when the man inside the boathouse decided to step back outside. Bad timing.

Ryerson hurled himself at the metal door. There was a howl of muffled rage as the intruder ran straight into the slamming door. The gun and a flashlight that had been in the man's hands clattered to the deck as he took the shock of the metal door on his right arm. The weapon skittered across the boards and plopped into the black water. The flashlight followed. The intruder reeled back inside the dark boathouse, clutching his injured arm.

"Don't move," Ryerson said softly. He stepped into the doorway, straining to see his victim in the darkness. He held the gun steady in his hand. "Not one inch."

The stranger stared at him for an instant, his face impossible to see in the shadows. Then he disappeared, leaping sideways out of the pale light seeping in through the open door.

"Damn."

So much for the Rambo approach. Ryerson jumped through the doorway. He had to move fast.

The stranger shot forward to meet him, and the two men collided in the shadows. They both landed with a solid thud on the wooden planking.

Ryerson thought about the possibility of a knife as he and the intruder rolled across the floor. Brigman had been killed with a knife, and the Toralina cops had said the job had been done by a man who knew what he was doing.

Both Ryerson and his assailant were fighting blind. Ryerson tried to slam his gun against the side of the man's head and struck a coil of rope, instead. Disgusted, he let go of the gun and concentrated on using his hands to win the silent, deadly struggle.

It didn't take good night-vision, merely proximity and desperation, to land several thudding blows. Ryerson absorbed two—one in the chest and one in the shoulder—before he got in a decent swing of his own. When he did manage it, he had the satisfaction of hearing something crack. His opponent grunted and heaved violently, trying to dislodge Ryerson.

The man was big. Big enough to shove Ryerson aside for an instant. Before Ryerson could grab him, he rolled clear. There was a scrambling sound on the wooden planking. Ryerson went still, fighting to control his breathing. He could see nothing and knew that his only advantage lay in the fact that the other man was equally blind.

He heard the heavy, gasping breaths in the darkness and followed the sounds closely, praying he was not giving away his own position with the same kind of breathing. Water lapped softly at the planking.

A board squeaked, and Ryerson felt the dock give slightly. The intruder was trying to find him in the darkness. Ryerson stayed where he was, striving to pinpoint his own location. Cautiously he put out a hand and found a metal toolbox. He knew where he was now, and he remembered the fishing net he had stored on the shelf next to the toolbox.

Silently he swept his fingers around in a short arc, seeking the net. Wood squeaked again, and the heavy breathing came closer.

Ryerson's fingers closed around the net. He moved slowly to a kneeling position, aware that the small sounds he was making were probably giving away his location. He had no choice. He couldn't get the leverage he needed while lying on his side.

"Got you, you bastard," the intruder hissed and closed in on the source of the small noise he had heard. Something heavy arced through the air not far from Ryerson's head. The man had probably snagged a hammer or wrench from a shelf.

He felt the man move in the darkness.

At the last instant, Ryerson slung the fishing net. It fanned out silently, enveloping its target in a mass of soft nylon.

The intruder swore furiously as the net settled around him. He yelled his rage and stumbled wildly about as he tried to shake himself free. The more he struggled, Ryerson knew, the more tangled he became.

Ryerson surged to his feet and stepped backward, once more seeking the shelving where he had found the net. This time his fingers closed around a large flashlight he kept there.

He grabbed the light and snapped on the beam. The intruder was flopping around on the dock, looking very much like a large fish caught in the net. He swore again and ceased his struggles as the light played over him.

Ryerson aimed the beam at the intruder's face. "Well, hell," he finally murmured. "You're not Ferris."

The stranger's eyes narrowed fractionally for a few seconds, and Ryerson knew he had recognized the name. It was not a reassuring thought. For the first time, he realized there might be more than one intruder on the island.

And Ginny was alone back at the cabin.

Ryerson picked up the rope on the shelf and went toward his victim with grim determination. He needed some information, and he needed it quickly.

"Is Ferris here with you?" he demanded with seeming casualness as he methodically went about the task of tying the intruder's hands and feet. One thing you learned when you owned a boat was how to tie good knots.

"Go to hell."

Ryerson spotted the gun he had brought down from the cabin. It was lying near a clam-digging bucket. He finished tying several strong, tight knots and then went to pick up the heavy weapon.

The intruder glared at him derisively, clearly not impressed by the gun. Maybe he sensed it wasn't loaded, Ryerson thought with an inner sigh. Or maybe he just figured Ryerson wasn't the kind to pull the trigger on a bound man. Either way, the fool was right.

But there were other threats available.

Ryerson planted one sneakered foot solidly against his victim's shoulder and started to push.

"Hey, what the hell . . . ?" The man gasped as he was rolled to within an inch of the dock. The cold, dark waters of the sound sloshed with lazy menace.

"The water's not that deep here yet," Ryerson said pleasantly. "The tide's only partway in. If you find your feet, you should be just barely able to stand with your chin above the surface. Until the tide comes in completely, that is. We have some really dramatic tides around here. In another half hour or so, the water will be a foot higher. That will be about seven inches too high for you."

"You can't do this!"

"I don't see why not." Ryerson nudged him a little closer to the edge of the dock. "If it's any comfort, you probably won't have to worry about drowning. This water's so cold that you'll be lucky to survive for more than thirty minutes in it. Hypothermia is the real threat here. Either way, if I'm not back fairly soon, you're in trouble."

"Damn you!"

"If you want to make sure I get back in time to do you any good, you'd better give me an idea of what I'm facing out there." Ryerson used his foot to edge the man's bound legs toward the water.

"Stop it, you bastard. You can't kill me and you know it."

"I'm not going to kill you. The water will do it. And you've got an option, don't you? All you have to do is tell me what's waiting for me out there."

The man's eyes blazed in impotent fury. "Ferris is on the island," he snarled. "We came ashore in two different places. My job was to take care of the boat so you couldn't use it to get away. Ferris went to check out the cabin. He was supposed to wait for me. We were going to go in together."

Ryerson switched off the flashlight and headed for the door.

"What about me?" the bound man demanded furiously.

Ryerson didn't bother to answer. He shut the door of the boathouse on his way out.

Virginia stood at the window for long moments after Ryerson had left. She knew there was little she could do, but she hated the helpless feeling of being the one who had to wait.

After several agonizing minutes, she saw a figure emerge from the cruiser and go into the building. Her palms were damp. Perspiration trickled down her side under the robe. She leaned forward intently. An instant later, she saw another large, solid shadow step out of the trees. Ryerson. He was leaping for the metal door.

And then, without any warning, both men disappeared inside the boathouse. Ryerson had gone in after the intruder.

Virginia jerked free of the temporary paralysis that gripped her. She had to help Ryerson.

Racing for the bedroom, she found her jeans and a shirt. She pulled the clothes on, not bothering with more than one or two buttons on the shirt. The long sleeves dangled around her wrists. She fumbled with her shoes, and then she let herself out the front door, heading for the path that led to the boathouse.

She stumbled in the darkness, barely able to discern the narrow path in front of her. Frantically she grabbed for a pine branch to steady herself before she lost her balance.

She had just managed to catch herself when a man loomed up out of the shadows behind her and jerked her to a halt with an arm around her throat.

"Well, well, well," Dan Ferris murmured in her ear. "If it isn't the lady with the sexy wardrobe. The water around here is a little colder than it is down on Toralina, isn't it, Miss Middlebrook?"

"Ferris," she whispered, barely able to speak because of the muscular arm holding her still. She was pressed back against his body. She could smell the sweat on him.

"That's right. Dan Ferris. You and Ryerson have given me nothing but trouble, lady. You know that? I nearly lost you both after you left Toralina. Took me a week to find you. Then I had to bribe the guy who owns the marina on that other island to find out where you were. I've had it with both of you. Come on. Since you're out here running around in the darkness, I have to assume Ryerson is, too. Let's go find him."

"He's not . . . he isn't . . ." The arm tightened around her throat and Virginia felt something cold and sharp touch the side of her neck. She trembled, remembering that Harry Brigman had been killed with a knife. "What do you want from us?"

"The bracelet, for starters. After that, Miss Middle-brook, the most important thing I want from you and your lover is silence." He half dragged, half shoved her down the uneven path.

She knew then that Ferris meant to kill her and Ryerson. The bracelet burned on her wrist under the long sleeve of her shirt. She wondered what Ferris would do if he knew she was wearing it.

Ferris dragged Virginia to the clearing in front of the boathouse and then, holding the knife to her throat, he called out loudly.

"Seldon? You in there? What's going on? I've got the woman."

There was silence for a long moment. Virginia felt the dangerous tension in her captor. The knife tip pressed against her throat. She closed her eyes briefly and prayed that Ryerson was safe.

"Seldon!"

There was a groan from inside the boathouse. "I'm in here. Tied up. Ryerson's out there somewhere. Watch out for him, Ferris. The bastard's fast."

Ferris swore viciously and started to yank Virginia back into the safety of the trees.

"That's far enough, Ferris. Let her go." Ryerson stepped out from the shadows on the far side of the boathouse. Moonlight gleamed on the gun in his fist.

The rain had stopped. There was enough moonlight now for Virginia to see her lover's face, and what she saw stunned her. There was nothing in his expression of the indulgent, home-and-hearth, Mozart-loving man she had come to know so intimately during the past few weeks.

Violence vibrated in the air, and the knife dug a little more deeply into Virginia's throat.

"Let her go?" Ferris scoffed coldly. "Now why should I do that? Miss Middlebrook is my insurance policy. If you think you're good enough to shoot me without hitting her, you're welcome to try. There are very few men who are that good with a gun, though, Ryerson. Odds are you'll kill her, and you know it. Put down the gun."

Virginia looked at Ryerson and shook her head. "He's going to kill us both, anyway," she said with a calm that amazed her. "So take a chance."

Ryerson ignored her. "What do you want, Ferris?"

"I already told your woman what I want. The bracelet and your silence."

"We'll give you both if you let her go."

"Sure you will," Ferris said scornfully. "You're a businessman. You'll understand my wanting a little more insurance than just your Boy Scout word of honor. Now put down that gun before I put this knife into her throat."

Ryerson slowly lowered the nose of the weapon and took a couple of steps forward.

"I said, put it down!" Ferris snapped shrilly. He dragged Virginia farther out of reach, edging back toward the dock.

"As soon as you let her go." Ryerson continued moving forward cautiously.

"I'm not going to let her go, but I'll be glad to start showing you how serious I am."

Ferris pressed the knife deeper into Virginia's throat. She shuddered. The bracelet seemed hotter than ever on her wrist, and she wondered why she was so aware of it. Unconsciously she moved one hand to the arm on which she wore the bracelet.

"Stop it," Ryerson said calmly. "I'll give you the gun." He held it out.

"Just put it down on the ground."

Ryerson tossed it onto the wet pine needles. "The gun's yours. Now let her go."

"Not a chance." Ferris started pushing his captive forward, apparently intent on getting his hands on the gun. He kept the knife at Virginia's throat.

The bracelet was practically setting fire to Virginia's wrist. Surreptitiously she unsnapped the catch, only half-aware of what she was doing. She caught the glittering thing as it slipped into her palm.

"Is this what you want, Ferris?" she asked softly. Emeralds and gold and the white fire of diamonds gleamed in the pale moonlight.

"The bracelet," Ferris breathed, astounded. "Give it to me, you bitch."

But Virginia's arm was already in motion. She hurled the bracelet toward the water. It shimmered for an instant in midair and then it sank beneath the cold waves.

"No, damn you, no! You *bitch*!" Ferris lashed out savagely with the knife, but Virginia was already throwing herself to one side. For once her size and build were a distinct advantage. She was big enough to pull Ferris off balance. The shifting pine needles underfoot aided her effort. Her violent action changed the direction of the knife stroke.

Virginia felt cold, slicing pain in her shoulder instead of her throat and then a thudding impact as Ryerson hit both Ferris and her with the full force of his weight.

She rolled free of the violent battle on the ground, sitting up to clasp shaking fingers around her injured shoulder. She squeezed the wound tightly, trying to ignore the pain as she watched Ryerson and Ferris struggling on the ground. She felt dizzy. When she shook her head, trying to clear it, she realized Ferris was almost on top of Ryerson's gun. Belatedly she staggered to her feet.

"No!" she screamed, launching herself toward the weapon. Horror struck her as she realized she was too late.

Ferris's fingers closed around the gun. He raised it quickly, aiming at Ryerson, who ignored the threat of the weapon. Ferris pulled the trigger.

There was a faint click, and nothing happened.

Before Ferris could recover, Ryerson had slammed a fist, his full weight behind it, into Ferris's jaw. Ferris slumped on the ground. The gun fell from his fingers.

Virginia stared first at the gun and then at Ryerson. Ryerson just looked at her as he staggered to his feet.

Virginia gazed back at him in numb disbelief. "It wasn't loaded?"

"I'm a businessman," Ryerson said dryly as he walked toward her. "I believe in statistics. A loaded gun is more likely to be used against its owner than it is against an intruder. Of course it was unloaded. I'm not a complete idiot."

"Why did you buy it in the first place?"

Ryerson exhaled heavily. "Because you seemed so determined to get a gun of your own. And because I didn't know what we were up against, and it looked as if the cops weren't going to be much help. And because I couldn't think of anything else practical to do to protect you. There. Satisfied? As you can see, it was a totally wasted exercise in machismo. The gun didn't do me any good at all."

Virginia's grin was a bit shaky. "Some guys are so macho they don't even need to use guns, Ryerson. Guess you're one of those." Then the dizziness overwhelmed her, and she crumpled forward into his waiting arms.

Ryerson caught her. "My God, he got you. The bastard stuck that knife into you. Why didn't you tell me you were hurt?"

"I was going to mention it," Virginia said apologetically.

ELEVEN

"Are you sure you're all right?" Ryerson asked for what must have been the hundredth time since the emergency clinic had turned Virginia loose with a few stitches and some pain pills. He was busy docking the boat as he spoke. "We could have gone straight home to Seattle. We didn't have to come back here this morning."

Virginia shook her head as she prepared to step out of the boat. She was still wearing the clothes she'd had on in the middle of the night. The sleeve of her shirt was bloodstained, and there was a small, neat white bandage on her arm. "I feel fine. My arm hardly hurts at all. Just a flesh wound, as they say in the thrillers. The important thing is to find the bracelet."

"We'll never find it, Ginny," Ryerson said patiently. "Face it, honey, it's long gone. No telling where it landed when you tossed it into the water last night. And the tide's gone out since then."

"It's too heavy to float out on the tide."

"Maybe. But it could easily have been covered up with sand or debris or seaweed. Don't count on finding it."

"You've got to have faith, Ryerson." She jumped off the boat and strode along the dock, studying the terrain revealed by the retreating tide. "That bracelet is ours. I know it is. We'll find it. We were meant to have it. It helped save our lives last night."

Ryerson finished securing the boat and walked toward her with wryly lifted eyebrows. "I'll admit your tossing it into the water made an interesting diversion. Ferris panicked."

"And you were ready to take advantage of his panic," Virginia concluded with a rush of feeling. "You were magnificent last night, Ryerson. Absolutely magnificent."

"You weren't so bad yourself," he told her dryly. "The bit with the bracelet was a real inspiration." The rueful amusement faded from his silver eyes. "Ginny, you'll never know how scared I was when I tried to make Ferris exchange the knife for my unloaded gun."

"Nonsense. You didn't look scared at all. You looked big and ruthless and very dangerous." She shivered. "Ferris was the one who was scared. I could feel it."

"Don't argue with me, Ginny," Ryerson retorted harshly. "I know what I was feeling, and the feeling was one of pure terror. It would have been too easy for him to have put that knife into your throat and then made a grab for the gun. When you got his attention with the bracelet and then pushed him off balance, you saved your own life and mine, too."

"Yours, too?" Virginia glanced at him curiously. "Oh, you mean because you would have tried to rush him at the last minute and he would still have had the knife."

"He could have gotten both of us with that knife. He was an expert, don't forget. The cops said so. I would have been an easy target because if I thought he'd killed you, I would have been insane. I wouldn't have been able to think clearly enough to do anything but get my hands around his neck. Which is probably not the best way to attack a man who's holding a knife," Ryerson concluded pointedly. "Do you know what it would have done to me to see you get your throat slit?"

She looked back at him and saw the raw emotion in his face. "Oh, Ryerson," she whispered, running lightly back down the dock to wrap her arms around him. "Don't think about it. We saved each other last night, and it's all over now. I love you so."

He held her tightly for a long moment, his face buried in her hair, his palms moving warmly on her back. "I love you, too, Ginny. More than anything else on this earth."

Virginia raised her head from his shoulder and smiled. "We did all right for an information retrieval manager and a diesel motor man, didn't we? Wait until my family hears the whole story." She glanced over the edge of the dock. "Oh, my gosh—*there it is*! There's the bracelet, Ryerson!"

Ryerson watched with gleaming eyes as she raced back along the dock and jumped down onto the sand.

Virginia kicked off her shoes and took two steps into the shallows. The bracelet was lying on a rock barely an inch below the surface.

"It's just been sitting here all night waiting for us to come back and find it, Ryerson!" she exclaimed triumphantly. There was no way she could have missed it. The morning sun was releasing the fire in the stones, and they shone up at her like small, glowing green and white suns. She reached down and scooped the old bracelet out of the water.

It dangled from her fingers, shimmering and glittering, and sparkling with drops of water. She laughed up at Ryerson. "It's ours again. We've found it. The thing belongs to us. I know it does."

Ryerson crouched on the dock and studied the links of emeralds and gold and diamonds in her palm. He said nothing for a moment, and then his eyes met Virginia's. "*Is* it ours?" he asked softly. "Now that we know Brigman, Ferris and Seldon stole it?"

Virginia's triumph disintegrated into disappointment as reality took over. She looked down at the bracelet and sighed. "You're right, of course. I don't know what got into me. Ever since you won it in that poker game, I've had the strangest conviction that this bracelet really does belong to us. It's as if we were meant to have it. Things have been going so well for us since then. We've fallen in love since we came into possession of this bracelet. It even helped save our lives last night. I can't bear to give it up."

"I know how you feel." Ryerson stood up and stepped off the dock onto the sand. He waited for Virginia to wade out of the water. As she came to stand in front of him, he smiled quizzically. "But do you really think things will change for us if the bracelet goes back to its rightful owner? I love you, Ginny. Nothing could change that."

Virginia closed her eyes briefly as a sense of deep serenity welled up inside her. The bracelet was beautiful, and she would always feel a sense of possession toward it, but the love she had found with Ryerson was far more important than any piece of jewelry could ever be.

She opened her eyes and smiled. "I love you, Ryerson. And you're absolutely right, as usual. Nothing could change the way I feel about you."

"Then we'll see if we can track down the rightful owner through that certificate of appraisal that we found in the box."

He put out his hand and Virginia slipped her fingers trustingly into his. The bracelet shimmered in Virginia's fingers as she walked up the path toward the cabin with Ryerson.

'I want to hear every detail," Debby Middlebrook announced two days later as she met Virginia and Ryerson for lunch. "I got most of the story from Mom and Dad, but I want to have it firsthand. Tell me everything, and start with how Brigman got the bracelet in the first place."

Virginia chuckled as she buttered a chunk of sourdough bread. She glanced at Ryerson, who was examining his salmon with grave interest.

"You tell her," Ryerson said. "I'm hungry." He picked up his fork.

"Ferris, Brigman and Seldon operated a theft ring that preyed on wealthy tourists who stayed in out-of-the-way locations in the Caribbean—places such as Toralina Island. It generally worked this way, according to the cops. Brigman was a professional poker player who usually engaged the male victims in a series of high-stakes games. Ferris entertained the ladies while their men were busy playing cards. Seldon stayed out of sight and did the dirty work. The three of them were careful not to be seen together so no one would make any connections after the thefts."

"Got it," Debby said enthusiastically.

"But the three men were basically business associates, not friends. Eventually there was, as they say, a falling-out among thieves. Ferris and Seldon began to suspect that Brigman was cheating them somehow, perhaps because he was in charge of fencing the jewelry. They were no longer sure he was splitting the take evenly."

"As it turned out, they were right to be suspicious," Ryerson put in around a mouthful of salmon. "Brigman had stolen the bracelet on his own. He didn't let his partners know about it."

"But Ferris and Seldon discovered the truth when they confronted him on the last night of our stay on Toralina. There was a violent quarrel, and Brigman wound up dead. Ferris used his knife on him, and Ferris is very good with a knife, as it happens. In fact, he apparently enjoys using it, according to the police." Virginia shuddered.

Ryerson picked up the tale. "Before Brigman died, however, he told his pals he'd lost the bracelet in the poker game with me. After Brigman's death, Ferris came looking for the bracelet in our room. Seldon wasn't so bold. He was nervous because of the murder. He decided to lie low."

"But Ryerson scared Ferris off that night in the hotel room?" Debby asked. "Even though Ferris had that knife and was apparently not afraid to use it?"

Ryerson grinned. "Ferris told the police that when he saw me come through the doorway with Ginny's travel-size hair dryer in my hand he thought I was holding a gun."

Virginia beamed proudly at him. "Ryerson was wonderful that night."

"Right. I covered myself in glory and a pink napkin," Ryerson agreed dryly.

"A pink napkin?" Debby glanced from one to the other with a puzzled expression.

"It's a long story," Virginia said hurriedly.

"I can imagine. You know, this whole thing is incredibly bizarre. I can't envision either one of you going through all these adventures. Neither of you seem the type, if you want to know the truth," Debby re-marked with sisterly bluntness.

"Love does strange things to its victims," Ryerson murmured. "I personally am looking forward to re-turning to my nice, normal, sedate existence. Ginny provides more than enough adventure in my life."

"So what happens now?" Debby demanded.

"Well," Virginia said slowly, "the police are not overly concerned with the bracelet. There's no record of it being reported missing on St. Thomas, which was where Ferris said it was stolen. In fact, the cops think Brigman might not have stolen it at all. They think he probably won it in a poker game, and that's why he decided he didn't have to share it with his pals. What-ever the truth is, the bracelet is ours now. But Ryerson is making some inquiries, which I'm hoping won't pan out. I love that bracelet."

Ryerson cleared his throat. "I was going to tell you, Ginny. I think I've located the owner. I got a message from the jeweler who did the appraisal this morning. I'm afraid it belongs to a Mr. and Mrs. George Gran-tworth of San Francisco. I'm going to phone them this afternoon."

Virginia exhaled regretfully. "Easy come, easy go, I guess. It was nice owning it for a while." She bright-ened. "You know, I'm rather curious about the Grant-worths."

Debby wrinkled her nose. "Why?"

"Because that bracelet is very special. I want to see what the owners are like."

"It's just a piece of jewelry," Debby remarked. "A beautiful piece, I'll grant you, but still—"

"It's not just a piece of jewelry," Virginia said forcefully. She looked at Ryerson. He smiled at her with his eyes.

"No," he said quietly. "It's not just a piece of jewelry. We'll go together to return it to the Grantworths in person. I'm curious about them, too."

George and Henrietta Grantworth were thrilled to learn that the bracelet had been found, and they were eager to meet the couple into whose possession it had fallen. Virginia and Ryerson took the morning flight to San Francisco on the following Saturday. A cab delivered them to an elegant old Victorian house in the expensive Pacific Heights area of the city.

"It does look like the sort of place where this bracelet would be right at home doesn't it?" Virginia noted wistfully as she walked up the steps beside Ryerson. She had a growing conviction that Ryerson was right. They had located the legal owners of the bracelet. Until now she had been hoping against hope that it was all a mistake.

"I'm afraid so," Ryerson murmured. He leaned on the doorbell. "Look at it this way. We'll feel virtuous about this for weeks to come."

"How dull." Virginia smiled wickedly. "One of the things I've been enjoying lately is feeling a little unvirtuous."

"Hussy."

"I packed the red teddy for tonight," she whispered.

Ryerson's eyes gleamed. He was about to comment when the door was opened by a neat, friendly woman in a housedress and an apron. She looked at them inquiringly.

"Yes?"

"Virginia Middlebrook and A. C. Ryerson. We're here to see the Grantworths. They're expecting us." Ryerson gave her his most sedately reassuring smile.

"Oh, yes. They're waiting for you in the living room. Come right in."

Two people rose in greeting as Virginia and Ryerson entered the beautifully restored Victorian room. Virginia liked them both on sight. If the bracelet had to be returned to anyone, then it might as well go back to these two, she decided. She studied them carefully as introductions were made.

Henrietta Grantworth was probably in her seventies, but there was an elegance about her that was ageless. It was obvious that she had been a beautiful woman all her life. Her silvery hair was done in a regal chignon, and her blue eyes were full of charm and intelligence.

Her husband was a distinguished-looking man a few years older than his wife. Virginia knew he must have been nearly eighty, but he carried himself with the confidence and energy of a much younger man. His thinning hair had once been black, and his dark eyes were alert and assessing. He extended his hand to Ryerson with obvious pleasure.

"Please sit down," Henrietta said. "I can't tell you how much we appreciate all the trouble you've taken to bring us the bracelet. It disappeared from our hotel room on St. Thomas several weeks ago. We notified the police on the island, but they let the matter drop once we left. When we checked again last week to see if there had been any progress, there wasn't even a record of our report. George and I assumed we'd probably never see the bracelet again."

"We've owned it for years," George said, glancing fondly at his wife. "Henrietta came into possession of it at about the time I first met her. She always liked to think it had something to do with our finding each other. She was very upset when it was lost."

Henrietta smiled warmly at Virginia. "I was just sick to think that it might have wound up in the hands of criminals. It wasn't meant for that kind of fate. But I should have known better than to worry. The bracelet always finds its way into the proper hands."

"What do you mean?" Virginia asked as she slowly withdrew the jewelry box from her purse.

George chuckled and looked at Ryerson. "Henrietta has always been convinced that the bracelet is rather special. Not just because of its intrinsic value but because it has enjoyed a very romantic history. It always seems to end up belonging to people who are very much in love. My wife inherited it from a cousin who fell in love with her husband shortly after she had inherited the thing from her grandmother, who claimed the bracelet was responsible for her own happy marriage. And so on."

"The stories go back for several generations," Henrietta said firmly. "And I'm sure they're all true. There's a legend attached to the bracelet. Supposedly it belonged to an aristocratic French family by the name of Montclair. It was part of a set that was broken up during the French Revolution. I don't know what happened to the other pieces, but I do know that whoever has come into possession of the bracelet has enjoyed a great deal of love and happiness."

Virginia was enthralled. "The bracelet has always been owned by lovers?"

Henrietta nodded quickly. "Sooner or later, it's always turned up in the possession of two people who fall in love and marry. George laughs when I tell the story, but the truth is, I think he believes just a little in the legend himself, don't you, dear?"

George smiled lovingly at his wife. "A smart man does not argue with good fortune, my sweet." He picked up her delicately boned hand and kissed her fingers. "And there is no doubt but that I have been a very fortunate man."

Virginia watched the elderly couple, aware of a deep longing in her own heart. This was the way it should be, she thought with sudden clarity. This was what she wanted with Ryerson: a lifetime of shared love and happiness.

She glanced at Ryerson and saw that he was watching her with an unreadable gaze. She turned back to

Henrietta Grantworth. "I'm glad the bracelet belongs to you," she said in a small rush of emotion.

"Thank you, my dear." Henrietta opened the box and gazed down at the bracelet. She was silent for a long moment, and no one broke the silence as she studied the contents of the box. When she looked up at last, she looked straight at Ryerson. There was a suspicious dampness in her clear blue eyes. "The bracelet has always been associated with love and marriage," she whispered.

Ryerson reached out and caught Virginia's fingers. He smiled down at her. "We may not have had it in our possession for long, Mrs. Grantworth, but I can assure you, it was very definitely associated with love while it was ours."

"Yes," Henrietta said. She closed the box with a decisive movement. "I can see that." Her eyes twinkled as she flicked a quick glance at her husband. "It definitely seems to have been associated with love. But what about marriage? I must warn you, Mr. Ryerson, the men who come into contact with the bracelet inevitably wind up offering marriage."

Virginia's fingers were nearly crushed in Ryerson's large palm as he smiled at Henrietta. "All the men in the legends have wound up offering marriage?"

"Oh, yes," Henrietta assured him. "All of them. Of course, up until recently there wasn't much option for an honorable man who found himself in love. He did the right thing by his lady. Not like today when a man thinks he can have his cake and eat it, too."

Virginia blushed at the familiar words. It was not so long ago that Ryerson had said something very similar to her.

"A lot of things have changed in the past couple of hundred years, Mrs. Grantworth," Ryerson said smoothly. "Today it isn't always the man who tries to wriggle out of marriage."

The grandfather clock in the corner chimed in the silence that followed his comment. Virginia suddenly found herself the focus of three pairs of interested eyes. She looked first at George Grantworth, who was watching her with indulgent humor and a curious understanding. Then her gaze slipped to Henrietta, who was studying her with an expectant expression.

Virginia turned to Ryerson. He was contemplating her with that same unreadable look she'd noticed on his face earlier. She swallowed cautiously and made her decision.

"Well, Ryerson," she said briskly, "when are you going to do the honorable thing and make an honest woman of me?"

Ryerson grinned, relief and happiness heating the silver in his eyes. He pulled Virginia into his arms, hugging her fiercely. "Just as soon as we can get a license, honey."

George Grantworth chuckled. "I know how you feel, Ryerson."

"You must allow my husband and me to give you your first wedding gift," Henrietta Grantworth said with quiet certainty. She smiled and held out the jewelry box to Virginia.

Virginia turned in Ryerson's arms, totally astounded. "The bracelet? Oh, no, Mrs. Grantworth. We couldn't possibly accept it. It belongs to you."

"The bracelet has a way of choosing its proper owners. I'm convinced that it was destined to belong to you. George and I have everything we need or want. Nothing will ever alter our love for each other. Something tells me that it's time the bracelet went on to another couple, and I believe you and Mr. Ryerson are the lovers it was meant for this time around."

"But, Mrs. Grantworth," Virginia began rather feebly. "It's too valuable to just give to strangers."

"The true value of the bracelet cannot be expressed in monetary terms. I think you know that as well as I do. I give it to you with my blessing and the hope that you will be as happy as George and I have been."

Ryerson tightened his grip on Virginia. "It's all right," he said softly. "We can accept it. It's ours."

Virginia heard the certainty in his voice and knew that he was right. Her fingers closed around the box. It seemed to her she could feel the warmth radiating from within. "I don't know how to thank you, Mrs. Grantworth," she whispered.

Henrietta laughed. "Don't thank me. The bracelet has a will of its own. I'll tell you the truth, my dear. I knew the minute I opened the box and looked at it that it was no longer mine. It belongs to you now. I'm sure of it. Far be it from me to interfere with destiny."

"You know," George Grantworth said easily as he rose to pour a glass of sherry for his guests, "I've always thought it might be interesting to track down some more of the history of that bracelet. Never got around to it myself, but you two might want to give it a whirl. Should be interesting."

"Where would you start?" Ryerson asked curiously as he accepted his glass.

"Why, France, of course," Grantworth said thoughtfully. "I had that crest traced once out of curiosity. The Montclair family has an ancient history in France. Apparently there was once a castle. Probably nothing left of it by now, but you never know."

A week later Virginia tumbled an armful of travel brochures down onto the turned-back bed in Ryerson's condo and stretched out beside them. She was wearing the scandalous red teddy, the bracelet and a plain gold ring.

"A castle," she breathed. "A real castle. It's still there after all these years. What a perfect spot for a honeymoon. The brochure says, and I quote, 'The famous Montclair castle has been turned into a first-class luxury hotel catering to those who seek relaxation as well as fine accommodations in the French countryside.' Just think, Ryerson—French wine, French food and French clothes."

Ryerson folded his arms behind his head. "Don't tell me you're going to spend our honeymoon shopping for clothes."

"The French," Virginia informed him gravely as she looked up at him from beneath her lashes, "are famous for designing the world's sexiest lingerie."

Ryerson grinned. "Is that right?"

"I have it on the best authority."

"Ah. Well, in that case," he said as he pulled her down across his chest, "I think we can include a shopping expedition on this trip to France. You were born to wear sexy underwear."

"What about you?" Virginia asked with a soft laugh.

"Me? I was born to take it off you, of course." He slipped the satin straps of the red teddy off her shoulders. He paused as she nestled closer. "Ginny?"

"Hmm?" She was toying with the crisp, curling hair on his bare chest.

"No second thoughts or regrets?"

She knew he was referring to the simple wedding ceremony they had gone through that afternoon. "No second thoughts and no regrets," she whispered, very sure of her answer. She lifted one hand to touch the side of his hard face. "I've been waiting all my life for you, A.C. It just took me a while to realize what I'd been waiting for."

Ryerson saw the love and certainty in her eyes, and his own gaze blazed with satisfaction. "The waiting is over. For both of us." He reached out to turn off the bedside lamp. Then he found Virginia's mouth and took full possession.

The Montclair bracelet glowed in the shadows, promising a lifetime of love and happiness.

New York Times bestselling author

JAYNE ANN KRENTZ

Legacy

A story of two unlikely lovers

Honor Mayfield thought that her chance
meeting with Conn Landry was a stroke of
luck. Too late she realised she was falling for
someone who was seeking to avenge a legacy
of murder and betrayal.

"A master of the genre...nobody does it better!"
—Romantic Times

**AVAILABLE IN PAPERBACK
FROM FEBRUARY 1997**

New York Times bestselling author

JAYNE ANN KRENTZ

Full Bloom

Part bodyguard, part troubleshooter, Jacob Stone
had, over the years, pulled Emily out of countless
acts of rebellion against her domineering family.
Now he'd been summoned to rescue her from a
disastrous marriage. Emily didn't want his
protection—she needed his love. But did Jacob
need this new kind of trouble?

"A master of the genre...nobody does it better!"

—Romantic Times

**AVAILABLE IN PAPERBACK
FROM MAY 1997**

DEBBIE MACOMBER

THIS MATTER OF MARRIAGE

Hallie McCarthy gives herself a year to find
Mr Right. Meanwhile, her handsome
neighbour is busy trying to win his ex-wife
back. As the two compare notes on their
disastrous campaigns, each finds the perfect
partner lives right next door!

*"In the vein of When Harry Met Sally,
Ms Macomber will delight."*

—Romantic Times

**AVAILABLE IN PAPERBACK
FROM SEPTEMBER 1997**

CAROLE
MORTIMER

Gypsy

She'd always been his one temptation...

Shay Flannagan was the raven-haired
beauty the Falconer brothers called Gypsy.
They each found her irresistible, but it was
Lyon Falconer who claimed her—when he
didn't have the right—and sealed her fate.

**AVAILABLE IN PAPERBACK
FROM SEPTEMBER 1997**

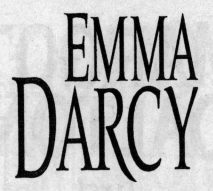

EMMA DARCY

*at her most daring with an
unforgettable tale of ruthless sacrifice
and single-minded seduction*

THE SECRETS WITHIN

When Tamara Vandlier learns that her mother is
dying she is elated—and returns to the family
estate to destroy her mother's few remaining
months, in return for her own ruined childhood.
Loyalty turns to open rivalry in this novel that
explores the dark, hidden secrets of two branches
of a powerful Australian family.

**AVAILABLE IN PAPERBACK
FROM AUGUST 1997**

Take 3 of
"The Best of the Best™"
Novels FREE
Plus get a FREE surprise gift!

Return this coupon and we'll send you 3 of "The Best of the Best" novels
from MIRA® books and a surprise gift absolutely FREE! We'll even pay
the postage and packing for you. We're making this special offer to
introduce you to some of the world's very best romance novels written by
the world's very best romance authors. Accepting these free books and
the gift places you under no obligation to buy any further books.
You may cancel your subscription anytime, even after receiving just your
free shipment.

REPLY TODAY - NO STAMP NEEDED!

THE BEST OF THE BEST, FREEPOST, CROYDON, SURREY CR9 3WZ
Readers in EIRE send coupon to PO Box 4546, Dublin 24

YES, please send me 3 FREE Best of the Best novels and a free surprise
gift. I understand that unless you hear from me, each month I will receive
3 of the best books by the world's hottest romance authors for only £3.75
each*. That's the complete price and a **saving of 25%** off the combined
cover prices. Postage and packing is completely free. I am under no
obligation to purchase any books and I may cancel or suspend my
subscription at any time, but the free books and gift will be mine to keep
in any case. (I am over 18 years of age)

B7YE

Ms/Mrs/Miss/Mr _____
BLOCK CAPITALS PLEASE
Address _____

_____

_____ Postcode _____

THE BRIGHTEST STARS IN WOMEN'S FICTION

MIRA

LINDA HOWARD

ALMOST FOREVER

THEY PLAYED BY THEIR OWN RULES...

She didn't let any man close enough.

He didn't let anything get in the way of his job. But Max Conroy needed information, so he set out to seduce Claire Westbrook.

BUT RULES WERE MEANT TO BE BROKEN...

Now it was a more than a game of winners and losers. Now they were playing for the highest stakes of all.